WITH DANGEROUS

AIM

By Harold Adler

ARPress
45 Dan Road Suite 5
Canton MA 02021
Hotline: 1(888) 821 0229
Fax: 1(508) 545 7580

Ordering Information:
Quantity sales. Special discounts are available on quantity purchases by corporations, associations, and others. For details, contact the publisher at the address above.

Printed in the United States of America.

ISBN 13:   Paperback   979-8-89356-889-9
              Hardcover   979-8-89356-891-2
              eBook   979-8-89356-890-5

Library of Congress Control Number: 2024909045

Novels by Harold Adler

Alone on Watch

Mantle of Spies

On Dangerous Water

Contents

AUTHOR'S COMMENTS

With *Dangerous Aim* is a work of fiction. The names of the characters and incidents portrayed in this novel are the author's creativity. Any resemblance to an actual person, companies or naval events are coincidental. Anchors Aweigh.

CHAPTER ONE

Dusty offered a half-smile as he entered his boss's office. The director, who was having a heated conversation on the phone, watched Dusty slowly waltz into his office and pointed for him to take a seat. Dusty was promoted becoming the senior operations manager at the Alexander Hamilton Foundation. His next task was to make sure she surreptitiously escapes from China. He would be in charge of the satellite trajectory for this operation as well as human- intel. He was not wet-behind the ears when it came to intelligence work. He had ten years of clandestine experience and was ready for this key assignment. He had one lingering problem; he was to coach two rookie mules in Shanghai, China in this operation as well as ask the U.S. Navy for support. Dusty was worried the two inexperienced untested undercover agents might blow the assignment. Failure was not in his lexicon.

The director finished his phone call and commented as he gazed at Dusty,

"Familiarity breeds contempt."

"What do you mean by that?" asked Dusty Sommers as he leaned forward and squinted his eyes trying to understand the phrase.

Theo Von Laube, the aged and white-haired Director of the Alexander Hamilton Foundation, was about to explain when he answered his phone, again.

As Dusty tried not to listen to the conversation, he looked down at the gray carpet when his mind wandered back to his younger years as a senior in high school where he played a practical joke during Halloween. He picked up a roll of toilet paper from the bathroom and went outside near the two-lane county road several blocks from his house. Dusty unraveled the paper into a rough-looking twine. He coiled it up as the toilet paper now looked like thin white rope. He stretched it across the country road and tied each end to a tree. He remembered he gently pulled the paper taught as it now appeared to look like half-inch rope stretched across the road at night. He chuckled to himself and could not wait until a car approached the fake rope. He waited in the bushes and saw a car approaching his roadside prank. The car noticed the white line stretched across the road and flashed its bright lights to get a definite observation on this white line three feet high hovering over the road. All of a sudden, Dusty heard the car's tires squeal on the road to a quick stop a few feet from the apparent rope. He saw the driver get out of the car and walked over to the rope. He touched the rope and knew it was only paper. He pulled on it and the paper fell apart. Dusty watched as the driver looked around searching for the villains who played this prank and then he got into his car and drove away. Dusty chuckled a few more times and tied the paper together and waited for the next car to see the rope stretched across the road. Waiting in the bushes twenty feet away, he saw another car flash its bright lights seeing the rope across the road. Dusty saw the car swerve on the road to miss hitting the rope. The approaching car flew into the ditch and stopped. The driver got out of his car and walked over to the rope. He tugged on the rope and instantly knew it was only paper. He looked around searching for the culprit who pulled this mean prank. Dusty could not contain his laughter. The driver heard the distant laughter and took off running toward the noise. Dusty saw the man running toward him. He quickly got up and his laughing young voice turned into fright as he heard the driver yell, 'I'm going to get you and beat you, you little creep.' Running away at full gallop in the dark, Dusty could hear the running footsteps behind him grow closer. Fortunately, Dusty knew to jump over this three-foot deep ravine and keep running as fast as he could to pull away from this irritated driver. The driver did not know of the ravine nor could he see the ravine in front of him in the dark. The driver fell chest first onto the muddy slope of the ravine losing his momentum to grab the little night weasel. Dusty could hear the man shout, 'I'll get you!' Dusty kept on running to circle around back to his house. He sat smiling from his past event in his younger life. His smile disappeared when he saw the director hang up the phone.

The director continued, "When one repeats the same job over and over throughout the years, as I have, one will make simple mistakes, thus people get killed, which is bad for our business. You don't want to become numb at the job. Numbness breeds anger. Besides, I've been here at the Hamilton Foundation for too many years. I should have removed myself from the spy business ten years ago."

"Oh, I see."

"Not too many people know this, although the board of directors know, when I was in the army during WWII in northern Africa, the Office of Strategic Services also known as the O.S.S. was conducting interviews for their clandestine services to work behind enemy lines. They needed German-speaking people to blend into the German lines. I wanted out of Africa, gosh there were flies all around us. I hated Africa. Having a German background, they evaluated you to see if you act like a German and talked fluently like a German. As I was from New Braunfels, Texas, a German community. Easily, I passed their tests. They said, there was one more test."

"What was the next test, Director?" Dusty took a sip of his coffee listening intently.

Von Laube grinned and gently scratched his clean-shaven face, "Dusty, this brings back some old memories." He looked straight into

Dusty's young eyes and continued. "They took you to an airfield and placed a parachute on your back. There were four of us who boarded the airplane. They gave us instructions on jumping."

Dusty asked, "Where were you going?"

The Director leaned back in his chair and explained. "They parachuted us behind German lines near Tobruk, which the Germans held. We flew over the Mediterranean Sea hoping the Luftwaffe didn't shoot us down. Then we turned toward our destination. The northern coast of Africa. At night, we jumped out of the airplane at 2,500 feet. I quickly pulled the ripcord and I was jerked hard by the opening parachute. It was a quick trip back to earth. Once I landed on the sandy ground, I buried my parachute and made my way into Tobruk and hopefully walked my way out and back to the American or British lines. This was the test to become an O.S.S. agent. They said, 'Don't get caught, you'd be shot as a spy.' At this point, I knew they were not clowning around."

"I'll bet that was scary?" Dusty asked.

"Oh, not really. I had all the confidence of a German. I wasn't afraid. Of course, I was wearing a German Officer's uniform, which gave me an advantage behind the lines."

"What was your German officer's rank?"

"I held the rank of major. I was wearing the uniform of the Abwehr, which was the German military intelligence service. At night, I caught a ride to the front lines. At this point, it gets a little dicey. I asked who was in charge and where was the field headquarters. The German soldier was respectful and pointed the way to the headquarters. I walked into the tent and was immediately greeted by the Ober Gruppen Fuhrer, which is the senior military leader."

"I see,"

"I immediately informed the Ober Gruppen Fuhrer. I was to walk out into the open desert to find my way to the American or British lines. Once there, learn of their number of tanks and men for Rommel's next offensive push. He wanted to call his General and inform him of my doing. I told him there would be no call to his general since this was all secret. So, I asked him if he had any cognac, since I might not make it back. He smiled and reached for the hidden cognac bottle and we had a toast to our Fuhrer. Then he asked me how I arrived in Tobruk. I looked him straight in his eyes and said they flew me from Rome, Italy. I parachuted a few miles from here."

"Obviously, you made it back to the friendlies."

"It was tough walking at night in the sand. With each step, you would sink a good inch into the soft sand. Fortunately, it was a clear night, one had to look above at the stars so you would not lose your direction toward the American lines." The director paused to pick up his cup of coffee and continued, "Well, enough of my past history." The director tapped the top of his desk and said, "Dusty, we are assigned to recover a treasure. She is a Chinese defector and assist her out of Shanghai, China, which should be easy."

"Who is this Person?"

"Her name is Ming-Li Yang. As I told you earlier, she has had enough of the Chinese government and requested to come to America. And I am placing you in charge of this mission and getting her out of China safely."

"Thanks for the job, but I was to begin my vacation next week. I guess I'll postpone my vacation. Are you sure, I can do this?" asked Dusty.

Director Laube took his gold-rimmed glasses off his face and placed them on his desk and he enlightened Dusty, "You have the chops for this mission. You have over ten years of intelligence experience. It's time you step up to the plate and play in the major league of the spy business. Sometime this morning, if you will, contact Admiral Mahone." The director reached for the Admiral's phone number and handed the slip of paper to Dusty.

"How can he help us?"

"First of all, the admiral is she. Admiral Janis Mahone. I have met her several times and she is very bright and competent with three stars on her shoulder boards. Admiral Mahone is our navy contact to help the lady out of Shanghai."

Dusty took another sip of his coffee and asked, "Who is our agent in Shanghai and how do I get in touch with him?"

"His name is Nick McMasters. He has been with us for six years. Nick works undercover at the U.S. Consulate General Office in Shanghai. Nick knows to meet his contact meet at the Shanghai Pudong International Airport. His contact will know where to rendezvous with Ming-Li. Much of the plan has been worked out. Here is the folder with all the names and phone numbers you'll need. Don't let this folder out of your sight. Lock it up in your safe at night. You'll just monitor the mission, all right? If there are any screw-ups, fix them. Use your keen sense of logic to get her safely out of Shanghai." The director stopped for a moment thinking. "Also do not let the British, the Japanese, or even the frogs know of this operation. Keep them all in the black."

Dusty looked intently at Director Laube and asked, "By the way, who is Ming- Li?"

Director Laube opened a folder and described Ming-Li to Dusty, "Ming-Li Yang has a degree from the University of Toronto, Canada. She earned a Ph.D. in Aerospace Science and Engineering. Presently, she is the head of the micro- satellites and cybersecurity for China. She became highly irritated with her government and chose our way of life in the West." The director stood up walking around his desk and tapped Dusty on his shoulder several times. "Keep me advised on the mission, all right?"

"Yes, sir." Dusty asked, "Who were you talking to in Russian over the telephone?"

The director paused for a moment, thinking as his eyes remained glued to the dark carpet. His mind was searching for an answer. He was unsure how to answer Dusty. Should he tell him or not tell him?

He raised his head and asked, "Do you remember Albert Speer, who was Adolf Hitler's Architect and Ammunitions Minister during World War Two?"

"Sure."

"Well, we were in Mannheim, Germany in April of '45 waiting for Albert Speer to come out of his home. It was a cloudy chilly day. In this part of the neighborhood, nothing was bombed. We were waiting for him outside of his house. As he walked out of his house in the early morning, he greeted us. He knew the war was over. We greeted his wife and took him to a holding area. He was very much a diplomate. He was courteous and you could tell he was quite intelligent. We asked him when was the last time you visited your Fuhrer? He said a few days ago. He was in the bunker and he was probably dead. He said the Fuhrer was an idiot. He just whipped the German people up into a frenzy and they followed his national socialism like sheep. He said attacking the Russians was a huge mistake. Economically, Germany did not have the full resources to sustain a war. Speer said the Fuhrer did not understand economics. After the loss of over two hundred thousand army troops at Stalingrad, Hitler could not realize he made a mistake. At that point, Speer knew he was nuts. The Generals were afraid of him. They were afraid of being taken outside and shot. They did not have the courage to speak against Hitler. At the Nuremberg trials in forty-six, Speer was the only high-ranking German officer who said he was sorry, which probably saved his bacon. He was not hung or shot like a few generals were hung or shot. Speer spent twenty years at the Spandau prison outside Berlin. We smuggled out his writings. He turned his writings into a famous book, <u>Inside the Third Reich</u>, which you probably have read?"

Dusty stood with his arms folded across his chest listening intently to the director. "Yes, I have read his book."

"What I am about to say next is confidential, all right?" He waited for an answer from Dusty.

"Yes, sir."

"During the war, I was Herr Umdrehen or Mr. Turn About. I turned things around. I don't want this information to get out nor do we need the press here. The guy on the phone was my KGB counterpart. He is retired. I will not tell you his name. He lives quietly with his wife outside of Russia. Each Christmas, I send him a Christmas gift. Albert Speer was in London, England and died at the age of seventy-six in his hotel room. He was poisoned by the Russians. That information was kept quiet and that is all I'll say on the subject."

Dusty offered a half-smile and said, "Thank you for telling me, Director."

"Oh, make sure you don't tell anyone you are on this assignment. Too many people involved in the mission causes friction. Friction is what you don't need. If you talk to the other analysts about the operation, they might give you the wrong advice. You have to do your own thinking. The less people know about what you are doing, the better. As you know, if you have too many fingers in the pie, the pie will taste bad. Do you get my drift?" Director Laube gazed directly into Dusty's eyes. He saw a half-baked smile on Dusty's face and watched Dusty accompany his smile with a head nod. "Oh, one more thing, Dusty." The director grit his teeth together and asked, "Is that your beat-up truck in the parking lot with two bales of hay in it?"

"Yes, sir. It is."

The director shoved his hands into his pants pockets. "With this promotion, ah, maybe you could purchase a new vehicle? People around here are beginning to talk."

"We'll look into it, Director." Dusty turned away and walked toward his cubicle down the hall. The other lingering problem which was on Dusty's mind was his girlfriend, Dianne, who was having her parents from New York over for dinner the next day. He knew Dianne's parents did not like him. Dusty wasn't a lawyer or an investment banker as they wanted their daughter to live the high life as her parents were living. Dusty did not tell Dianne what he did at the Hamilton Foundation. He only told her he was the accountant for the firm. Since this assignment came up, he did not tell Dianne he might miss the dinner. Living on his 10-acre farm, her parents kept discouraging their daughter from seeing this Dusty character. Her father said she could do better. Dusty did not like her parents too much. Her mother continued calling her daughter every Thursday night telling Dianne she could ameliorate her position in life with a more refined gentleman instead of a local farmer. The other day Dusty tossed around in his mind to either purchase a used 1964 Massey-Ferguson tractor with an attached mower for the farm or a diamond ring for Dianne. He knew she would swim against the current to be by his side. Her parents only knew he worked for some unknown company. Dusty had been seeing Dianne for nearly a year. He was getting into debt with his credit cards. He purchased a new washer and dryer for his wooden frame house. The thirty-year-old three-bedroom house needed repair. The neat part of the farmhouse is that it had three red brick fireplaces. The plumber repaired the leak in the kitchen sink and installed new oak wood flooring throughout the house.

Dusty decided to either repair the roof of the house or the roof of the small barn. He spent six thousand dollars on a new roof on the farmhouse. He could save some money and repair the barn roof by himself. With a few four-by-eight plywood sheets, they would stop the rain pouring onto the dirt floor of the barn and turning the dirt floor into a one-inch pool of mud. He knew Dianne wanted a commitment from him. He decided to propose to her and offer a one-carat diamond ring. She enjoyed the working farm as well as being a newly minted MBA from Georgetown University. Dianne was going back for the second interview at a large trucking company.

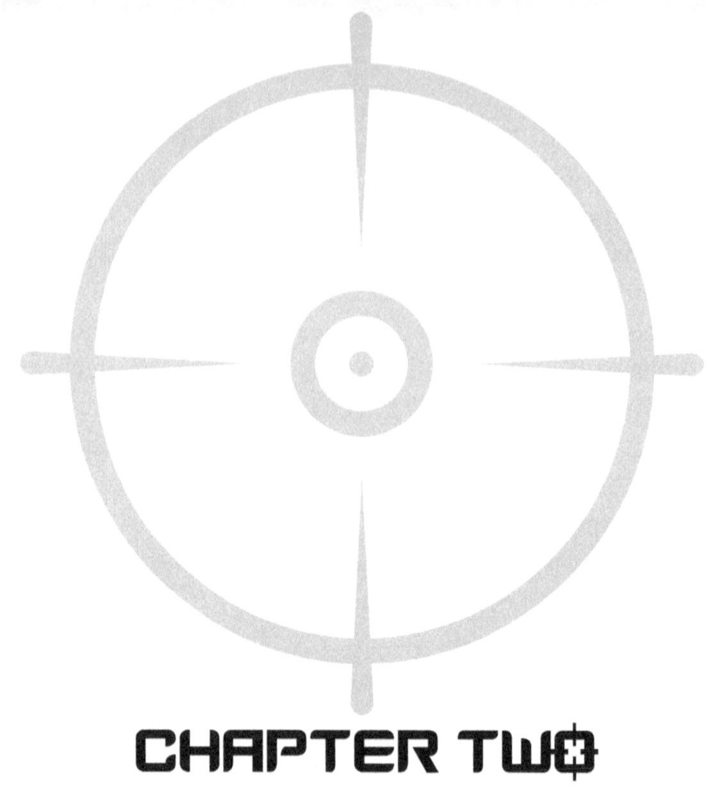

CHAPTER TWO

usty placed his personal problems away and concentrated at his desk. Dusty opened the secret folder. He recognized the names on the sheet of paper. Each person listed on the paper had top-secret clearances. The FBI already screened them. Dusty knew he had to collaborate with rookies on this assignment. The other covert agents in China were on other assignments and could not be used for this task. He recognized there might be a huge risk with two unproven agents in Shanghai. However, with two rookies moving about in Shanghai dodging the Chinese security team which might be following them, the untested agents would run like scared rabbits. Dusty knew with rookie agents if they had to run from the Chinese security team, the experienced security team would know how to chase an experienced agent, but they did not know how and where to chase- down an unexperienced agent. This was one advantage Dusty knew which was in their favor. Dusty wondered if he might need some assistance from the British to help push the Chinese security team away from the operation. Dusty realized, if spotted by the Chinese secret security team they would not know where and how to follow them, as they would know how to follow a trained agent running from the Chinese. Dusty took the risk with two inexperienced agents. He knew, this assignment in Shanghai needed to push forward. He looked down and concentrated on the list. The first name on the yellow sheet of paper was Admiral Janis Mahone's phone number. He punched in the phone number and waited for an answer. A yeoman answered the call and sent the call immediately to the admiral.

"Good morning Admiral Mahone this is Dusty Sommers from the Alexander Hamilton Foundation in Washington, D.C. "

"Morning Mr. Sommers. Director Von Laube said you'd be calling me. How can we help you?"

"Admiral, please call me Dusty." He listened to her reply. He noticed she had a soft but commanding voice for an admiral.

"No problem, Dusty."

"We are asking if you can place one of your submarines off the coast of Shanghai, China to pick up a guest for us?" Dusty's heart was beginning to pump a little faster waiting for the admiral's reply.

"We can do it Dusty. When do you request this operation?"

"This will be a quick pick up. I sent you the coordinates where the submarine can locate the package."

"Fine Dusty."

"Our operations department has already sent you the information we will need for this assignment. You should receive the package this morning by courier. We would like to have a Pacific Asian woman fly into Shanghai. We need a woman who can blend into their culture. She would meet with our agent, Nick McMasters, who works at the U.S. General Consulates office in Shanghai. Can you supply this Asian woman on this short notice? The pickup point is in the letter you should receive this morning."

"I think the courier is already here. Yes. My yeoman just received your package. That was fast." The admiral opened the envelope. "Yes, I believe we can have your Pacific Asian person for this assignment today. Dusty, can this person be a man or a woman?"

"I believe a woman would be a better touch for this assignment. Admiral, when you have the time, please call me with the agent you have selected for this assignment so I can give the name to Nick in Shanghai," Dusty paused, " if there is any disturbance in this operation, please let me know. It is imperative we get this assignment right."

"I understand Dusty. Is that all?" Admiral Mahone asked.

"Oh, one more thing. Please let me know when the flight from Tokyo departs. I can track the flight when it arrives in Shanghai. I can tell McMasters when he can meet her at the airport. That should do it, Admiral. Thank you for your help." Dusty placed the phone onto its cradle. He thought to himself, that went well. The next call would be to Nick McMasters in Shanghai.

CHAPTER THREE

Admiral Janis Mahone sat at her desk looking outside at the clear blue Hawaiian sky watching the leaves of the palm tree gently swing in the lazy wind wondering how the day was going to unfold. Her sharp eagle eyes glanced down at the secret package on top of her desk. She caught sight of this black fly walking on the rim of her coffee cup. She hated flies. She barked, "Clermont, do you have a fly swatter? There is a fly in my office."

Clermont, the Second-Class Yeoman, quickly walked into the admiral's office with a rolled-up newspaper for the admiral to swat the fly. "Here you are Admiral."

"Thank you, Clermont. Now, if the fly would just stay still for a moment." The admiral took hold of the rolled-up paper and quickly swatted the fly. She barked, "Got'em!" She looked up at Clermont with a pleasing grin.

"Well done, Admiral. Can I clean your coffee cup and get you another cup of coffee?"

"Yes, please. Oh, knowing you will be getting out of the navy in a month, have you selected a university?"

"Yes, I have. I've been approved to attend the University of San Diego."

The admiral smiled at Clermont saying, "I'm pleased to hear that. Can you call Lieutenant Commander Marshall in here?"

"Of course, Admiral." Clermont turned away and walked down the hall to Marshall's office. He poked his head into the office and said, "Morning Commander Marshall, the admiral is looking for you."

Pilar Marshall entered the admiral's office. She was an attractive naval officer with shoulder length black hair. She stood at five feet ten inches tall. She had an athletic build. She was slim but had noticeable curves on her body. Her smile was infectious. She could disarm anyone with that smile. She asked, "Admiral, I've been meaning to ask you, how was your ascent to become an Admiral? I'm sure it was not easy." Pilar sat down listening.

Admiral Mahone began to describe her naval career, "Although you have to look good on paper, it is your personality which comes into play, too. Climbing up from an ensign to a lieutenant was somewhat uneventful. There was one incident at sea when I was a lieutenant commander. As executive officer of the USS John S. McCain, we almost collided with a Japanese freighter, which I'll never forget."

"What happened?" Pilar sat on the edge of her chair intent on listening to her boss. Her eyes were focused as she crossed her legs ready for a history lesson.

"The incident happened on the midwatch about three or four in the morning. The skipper had retired to his quarters and I was in the wheelhouse with the helmsman watching this freighter a few miles away grow closer to us. I mentioned to the helmsman to slowly change course so we don't collide with the freighter on our starboard side. The skipper gave a standing order, if there is a change in course, let him know." Admiral Mahone sat back in her chair and took a sip from her coffee mug. "Well, the helmsman wanted to wake the skipper since we needed to make a course change. I said no. Do not wake the skipper. He remarked that we'll get into trouble if we don't tell him. By now, our destroyer and the freighter were one hundred yards apart. I told him to slow our ship down and slowly turn the ship to the left to avoid a collision. He wanted to sound general quarters waking up the entire crew. I said, no, don't do that. He was frozen at the helm and as of yet, had not steered the destroyer away from the freighter. We were headed on a direct collision point with the freighter. I hit the horn and the noise blasted the air alerting the oncoming freighter. The freighter did not change its course. The freighter should have yielded to our starboard and either slowed their forward knots or turned away. At this point in time, we were, I'd say, fifty yards away from hitting the freighter. The helmsman hit the button to sound the alarm for general quarters. I told the helmsman to stand down and I turned us away from the certain disaster. The destroyer completed a three- sixty degree turn to the left and in a few minutes, we were back on course. By now the skipper was up standing in the wheelhouse glaring at me."

Pilar was on the edge of her seat listening absorbed in the Admiral's story. "My lord, what happened next?"

"I announced on the 1MC to secure from general quarters. He thanked me regarding the courtesy of letting the crew secure from general quarters. He growled, why did we get the crew up? What is the reason, XO? I could see the helmsman was scared that he did not want to be reprimanded by the skipper. Before the helmsman had a chance to say a word to the skipper, I quickly said we were too close to the freighter and I gave a blast on the horn. The freighter remained on its true course. I turned the destroyer away from a collision and I wanted the crew to be prepared in case the freighter turned into us. I know I should have given you a heads-up about a course change, but it was a simple three- sixty turn to avoid running into the freighter. We are back on our true course. He began to dress me down in front of the midwatch crew. The one thing you don't do is reprimand a subordinate officer or even a petty officer in public. He yelled at me for a good five minutes. At this point, I knew this guy was a complete jerk. I had no confidence in him anymore. He had no leadership skills. So, while in our next port, I requested a transfer, which was immediately approved. I was so happy to leave that command. My detailer in Washington said, my next duty station was at the Pentagon working in the office of strategy and supply. The navy needed more officers and I was promoted to commander. I nearly resigned my commission because of the incident with the jerk on that destroyer. Serving five years at the Pentagon, I was transferred to the Netherlands working at NATO and receiving my fourth stripe as captain." The admiral took a sip from her coffee mug. "I guess I had the right grease to earn a silver star on my collar, so I became Admiral Mahone."

Admiral Mahone took another sip from her coffee mug explaining she received a call from Dusty Sommers who works at the Alexander Hamilton Foundation and they needed a Pacific Asian to pick up a person wanting to defect to United States.

Pilar's face lit up. "I see. If you recall, Dusty was my husband's best man. You met him at our wedding reception."

"Oh, yes. Small world," the admiral replied and asked, "Think you might like to assist in this clandestine operation?"

"It sounds interesting," Pilar remarked. "What would I have to do?"

"Simply fly to Japan and then to Shanghai, China on a commercial jet. Once there, the agent in charge will meet you and get you through the city. Only you would know of the contact point in Shanghai to contact the person who wants to leave China. I think you would be a perfect fit for this overseas work. What do you think?"

"Sounds interesting, Admiral. Would I where my navy uniform?"

"No, definitely not, Pilar, you would have civilian clothes with no military Identification."

"When will this operation begin?"

"This afternoon, Pilar."

"Oh, I see. That quick." Pilar turned her head and looked outside at the blue sky and swinging leaves of the palm tree. As she swung her head back to face the admiral Pilar asked, "Where would I meet this person and who is this person that needs to escape to the United States?"

Admiral Mahone looked down at the secret paperwork sent by courier this morning. She looked up at Pilar and commented. "You would land at Pudong International Airport in Shanghai and meet Nick McMasters, who is the agent in charge of the operation. Inform him of the pick-up point at the Shanghai Porcelain store in Shanghai. He'll take you there to pick up Ming-Li Yang. One thing in your favor is that you already know Mandarin." Admiral Mahone reached into the package to pull out a watch and handed it to Pilar. "Pilar, please take off your watch and replace it with this one. This particular watch with a black rubber strap will follow your every move in Shanghai."

"Why would I need to wear this watch?"

"The satellite will be able to track your movement in Shanghai via the watch. I believe the watch will beep when you reach the rendezvous point which is off the coast of Shanghai."

"Oh, all right." Pilar placed the black watch on her wrist. "Sure, I'd be willing." Pilar started to think the operation through. Her mind quickly drifted away thinking about her husband, Chester, who is currently at the naval base in Sasebo, Japan. She missed him. She had not seen him in two months. Pilar wanted to talk to him about this mission. She began to have her doubts about this offer Admiral Mahone proposed. She never did anything like this before. Maybe, the mission borders on too much like a cloak and dagger operation, with which she has no experience in this field. This operation without experience might be too risky.

Looking at the admiral, she asked, "So, how do we escape from Shanghai? I guess not at their airport?" Pilar listened to Admiral Mahone wondering if she would have the tenacity to make the rank of admiral. As the admiral talked about her various rolls in the navy, Pilar gazed at her three silver stars on the admiral's collars. She realized the admiral had good grease. Pilar asked, "Who are we picking up?"

The admiral replied, "Oh, her name is Ming-Li Yang. I don't know what she does in China. Pilar, you would need to wear dark slacks with a beige shirt with no jewelry. Only wear the watch I gave you. Also, dark color of shoes, too. Also, don't wear any makeup. You will need to blend into the Chinese population while you are in Shanghai for the day. Nick will get you to a small marina where you would motor out to the pick-up point offshore." She noticed Pilar's eyes as they looked down and away. Admiral Mahone noticed Pilar's fear of moving on this mission. "Pilar, are you having doubts about this assignment? You know, you don't have to do this."

Pilar looked up directly at Admiral Mahone and said, "I know, but I would like to talk to Chester about this. I would feel more comfortable letting him know where I am going."

"Unfortunately, Pilar." The Admiral paused and stated, "There can be no communications about this mission nor to anyone else. Only you, I, Nick McMasters and Dusty Sommers know of this operation. We want to control the communications and to telephone your husband." Janis stopped her talk and said, "The lines are unsecure. Someone might be listening to your conversation. The less people know of this mission the better the success. Wouldn't you agree?"

The Admiral watched as Pilar nodded her head yes.

Pilar asked, "Who will pick us up?"

"We have one of our submarines to surface and pick you up. More than likely, our navy seals will meet you," answered the admiral.

"One question Admiral, what happens if we get caught?" Pilar grit her teeth as her eyes locked onto the admiral's tanned face. Again, doubt was starting to creep into Pilar's mind.

Admiral Mahone looked straight into Pilar's black searching eyes. "Well, there is always that possibility, but they have done this extraction before without any problems. I would not worry about getting caught. Put that thought out of your mind. All right? If it did happen, go to the U.S. Consulate Office. Just tell the Chinese authorities you are there as a tourist visiting Nick." She watched Pilar nod her head. The admiral reached into the package and pulled out funds for Pilar's trip. "Pilar, here is $5,500.00 dollars. Get this amount exchanged into Yen when you arrive at the Shanghai airport. Don't worry about the receipts. You'll take commercial flights from Honolulu Airport to Tokyo and then on to Shanghai. Make sure you get a roundtrip ticket back to Tokyo. Obviously, you won't be coming back to Tokyo but if checked by the Chinese they will know you are a tourist for a couple of days visiting Shanghai." The admiral stared at Pilar with a small grin.

"Trust your adventure to China will be uneventful and we shall see you back here in a couple of days." She watched Pilar stand and exit her office. Admiral Mahone had her bases covered. The admiral got the operative who is Pacific Asian the Alexander Hamilton Foundation requested. She commented, "Oh, one more thing Pilar, while on this mission, play dumb. Don't reveal your intelligence. And when you see Nick, your password to him is Pecan and his password to you us Pie." She watched as Pilar nodded her head yes.

"Oh, one thing admiral, how do I recognize this person at the ceramics shop?"

"Good question, Pilar." The admiral looked though the paperwork she received and found the line item for recognition. She looked up and said, "Pilar, you'll spot her wearing sunglasses and a colorful scarf. Your password to her is Red, White and Blue. Also, the visual code for recognition is on a series of five. Meaning using your hand as a coded signal, for example, if I show my index finger to you, as a number one, what is your reply from your hand?"

Pilar thought for a moment and looked at her hand. "Four." She displayed four of her fingers. "It represents the number five."

"Right. Now, you initiate a hand code back to me." Admiral Mahone glanced down at Pilar's hand.

Pilar exposed three fingers.

Admiral Mahone said, "How many fingers should I show you?"

"Two fingers." Pilar paraded two fingers to the admiral.

"Right. This is the other code Ming-Li will show you. If you get a different number. Walk away. You and Nick just get out of the store. At this point something went wrong. Abort the mission and head back to Hawaii."

Pilar nodded her head, yes.

"After you pick Ming-Li up, Nick will head you all to the rendezvous point. Got it? See you in a couple of days."

Pilar offered the admiral a half-smile as she turned and walked to her office. She saw the admiral give her a thumbs-up.

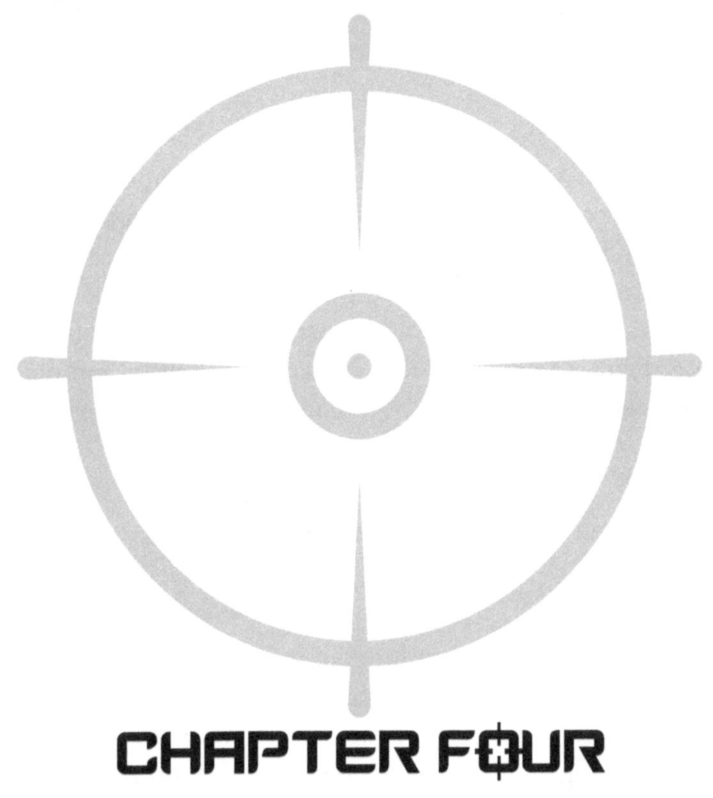

CHAPTER FOUR

Dusty hung up the phone after talking to Admiral Mahone. She gave him the name of the person for this assignment. Dusty printed the name of Pilar Marshall in his folder. He was pleased Admiral Mahone on short notice selected a Pacific Asian woman for this easy assignment. He was impressed to know Pilar had the courage to proceed with this operation. He wondered if his best friend Chester Marshall knew his wife was going to China. Anyway, the operation should be a relaxed one. Dusty knew with the solid caliber of Lieutenant Commander Pilar Marshall on this mission, there should not be any friction in pulling the escapee out of China. Dusty's next task was to locate the U.S. Consulate General's phone number in the folder. As the phone rang he reviewed the file on McMasters. He was an average midshipman and he was a graduate of the Naval Academy. Nick had been with the Alexander Hamilton Foundation for six years. While in Shanghai, Nick was monitoring the truck freight shipments at the port. He reached Nick. By listening to Nick's voice, which was a strong sounding voice, Dusty felt confident Nick could carry out this assignment with ease. Although Dusty would have liked to have a more seasoned agent for this operation, he believed Nick should be able to meet Lieutenant Commander Marshall at the Shanghai airport and then pick up the escapee taking them to the rendezvous point a mile off the coast of Shanghai. Just by listening to Nick over the phone Dusty felt sure Nick would not have any problems escorting the escapee out of Shanghai. Dusty felt he could trust Nick for this delicate stress-free assignment. "Good morning Nick, this is Dusty Sommers from Headquarters in Washington, D.C. I am the Operations Manager."

"Oh, good morning Mr. Sommers."

"Please call me Dusty, all right?"

"Sure. How can I help you?"

"We have an assignment for you. It is a laid-back one. I'm asking you to meet our person at the Pudong airport this afternoon. She'll be arriving from Tokyo. Her name is Pilar Marshall. She knows the itinerary in Shanghai. Once at the pickup point, you both will escort this person to an extraction location off the coast of Shanghai. Pilar knows the name of the store where the building is located in Shanghai, but she needs your help in getting her there. Just get her there and move out of the city to the extraction location. Pilar knows where this location is. She only needs your help to the coast. At this point, your job is completed and you can return to your normal duties as this assignment never happened. A piece of cake for you. How does this sound?"

"This should be an easy assignment. How do I recognize her at the airport?"

"She will recognize you since you are an American. There is a password for her to give you. Her password to you is Pecan and your password to her is Pie."

"Somewhat of a cloak and dagger type of a secret operation, huh?"

"You can say that. Nonetheless, this is a top-secret operation. It will be imperative we extract this person out of China nice and quietly. Do you understand?"

"Yes sir."

"All right, talk to you when you have completed this assignment." Dusty hung up the phone.

CHAPTER FIVE

After graduating from Shanghai University with an English and Business degree in logistics in warehouse planning, Candace Teng landed a position at a logistic warehouse in Shanghai. How she met Nick was by coincidence. She saw him standing on a busy street corner totally confused about which way to turn. She thought, another dumb American tourist. She watched Nick unfold a city map searching for a way out. Candace chuckled to herself observing this guy for 20 minutes, who is obviously lost in Shanghai. She noticed this guy was six foot tall having a good solid build on him and of course, he was handsome. Candace liked her man to be clean shaven. He was dressed in a relaxed business attire with a white short-sleeved shirt and dark pants. Candace enjoyed baseball and compared him to her idle, Harvey Kuenn, who use to play with the Cleveland Indians and was traded to the Detroit Tigers. She took pity on this lost tourist and she approached him, speaking English.

He was surprised she spoke English. They both settled on a cup of coffee nearby where she received an ear-full from this tourist.

Listening to him talk about the navy and then she learned he worked at the U.S. Consulate General office in Shanghai. Candace started to enjoy his warmth that this tourist was actually a friendly guy who was searching for a jewelry store to purchase a necklace for his aunt Alice back in the states. Candace definitely noticed the one-inch facial scar. The scar wasn't ugly but added character to his face. She wondered how he happened to received such a deep scar. The slice on his face did not bother her. She learned he was a graduate of the Naval Academy and was assigned to Shanghai. Candace was lonely. She did not date much. Candace was tired of living with her Mother and younger sister. The apartment was too small. She was tired of sleeping on the same old small couch night after night. She did not have a boyfriend although she had plenty of opportunities to have a boyfriend. Candace was searching for the right guy. She questioned if Nick's lips were strong. She did not enjoy sloppy wet kisses from a guy only strong passionate kisses. Instead of waiting for Nick to ask her on a date, Candace invited him to one of her nightly softball games. As a shortstop on the team, she would stand in the batter's box getting ready for the pitcher to throw the ball. Candace did not swing the bat like most other members on the team getting ready for the pitcher to throw the softball but would rotate the bat like a pendulum moving the bat slowly back and forth from left to right and back the other way in front of her knees as Harvey Kuenn would do when he was in the batter's box. When the pitcher was ready to throw the ball, Candace would swing the bat up ready for the pitch. Being 28 years old, Candace was tall and slender with shoulder length black hair. Candace had a playful smile. After a month of dating Nick, Candace moved into Nick's small one-bedroom apartment which overlooked a small park. The apartment was close to a bus stop where Candace could walk to and ride to her work, which was only twenty minutes away instead of the usual thirty- minute crowed bus ride. When she kissed Nick she leaned into him and wrapped her arms romantically around him. Nick's warm lips were strong. She could tell he was falling for her. She made sure he knew she loved him. She was content living with Nick. Her love for Nick was as strong as steel. He completed the necessary paperwork for a visitor's visa for Candace. She was surprised when he gave it to her for her birthday in July. Going to America was her dream. Her big dream was to leave

China, forever. She was making good money at her warehouse job but she could leave it in a heartbeat. Her best friend Margaret repeatedly told Candace not to trust this American. That he would only leave her when he transferred back to his next duty station. He would get you pregnant and leave you. Margaret hated Americans. She too was as attractive as Candace was. She worked with Candace at the freight company in Shanghai. Margaret believed Americans are greedy selfish people. She did not like Nick but tolerated him since he was in love with her best friend.

Nick enjoyed working at the U.S. Consulate Generals office but did not like working undercover keeping his work a secret from Candace and especially, Margaret. He reported his interest in Candace to the security department. The security team followed up by running a background check on Candace, her family and friends. Nick was pleased his girlfriend was given an all clear on her background check. That she wasn't a Chinese spy. Nick knew Candace was attractive with smooth clear complexion with dark serious eyes. Candace's soft-spoken voice always commanded Nick's attention. Nick often asked himself what was this brilliant girl doing with him. She had the power over him by her athletic build. More specifically, Candace had a pleasing way for him to gaze at her attractive body revealing her slender charms. To be more exact, her assets are what kept Nick coming back for more passion and pleasure.

At lunchtime on this sunny August day Nick returned to his apartment with a few flowers for Candace. She took the day off from work and was surprised by his return with colorful flowers. Nick asked, "What's for lunch?"

As Candace placed the flowers into a slender glass filled with water, she commented, "Well, we have some bread with cheese some fruit and sardines." Candace pulled the cheese and fruit from the small icebox. She looked at Nick asking, "I don't think you want any sardines, do you?" She saw him shake his head no. "I can make some brown rice if you like?" She noticed his return to a no response. "I have to go to the market to purchase more food today. I don't like to go on Saturday because the market is too crowed." Candace kissed him and thanked Nick for the flowers. As he wrapped his arms around her, Candace winced.

"What's wrong?"

Candace turned around and asked, "Can you pull up my shirt?"

"Why?" Nick asked as he gently pulled her shirt up onto her shoulders. He saw a number of long scratches on her back. "What happened?"

Candace turned around placing her arms on top of his shoulders saying, "The next time we make love, take your watch off. Your clasp from your watch dug into my skin."

"Oh. Sorry. Has my book arrived?" Nick peeked into the small bedroom to see the bed was made. Usually, Nick would have to make-up the bed.

"Surprised?" Candace grinned and remarked, " Yes, I made the bed up and yes your naval architect book arrived today." She handed the book to him. Candace asked, "By the way, why are you here for lunch? You usually eat lunch with your friends at work. Don't you?"

He flipped through the pages of the book and then set it down. "I have to pick someone up at the airport." There was a knock-on Nick's apartment door. Nick was not expecting anyone.

Candace looked at Nick saying, "That must be Margaret. She is going with me to the market."

Nick remarked, "Good. You two go to the market while I go to the airport."

Candace swung open the door and greeted Margaret with a hug. "Hi Margaret. Instead of going to the market, we are going to the airport to pick up Nick's friend. Then we can go to the market and do our shopping. All right?"

"Hi Nick," Margaret quickly commented. As she looked at Candace, "Sure." "Who?" she quickly asked.

"This lady is coming in from Tokyo." Nick did not want to tell Candace too much information about the arrival of this lady since her arrival was confidential.

"I'm going with you to the airport."

"That's all right. I can get there on my own," Nick answered.

Candace shook her head saying, "No you can't. You'd get lost. I'm going with you." Candace instantly searched for her visa for some odd reason to take it with her to the airport. "When is this person arriving?"

"Well, we should leave now." There was weight on his shoulders. He had to meet this person and shuffle her to a particular unknown location in Shanghai today. Nick remarked, "Good. You two go to the market while I go to the airport." Nick forced a grin saying, "Hi Margaret." He tolerated her. He could see daggers in her eyes every time she greeted him. He thought great, a huge parade going to the airport. The Chinese security team will surely notice us. Nick turned to Candace and asked, "Are you sure you want to go to the airport? I can get there by myself."

Candace took hold of Nick's arm. "Nick, you'd get lost. No. We are going with you to meet your friend."

Nick turned to exit the apartment gritting his teeth and mumbled, "Wonderful. This ought to be… fun."

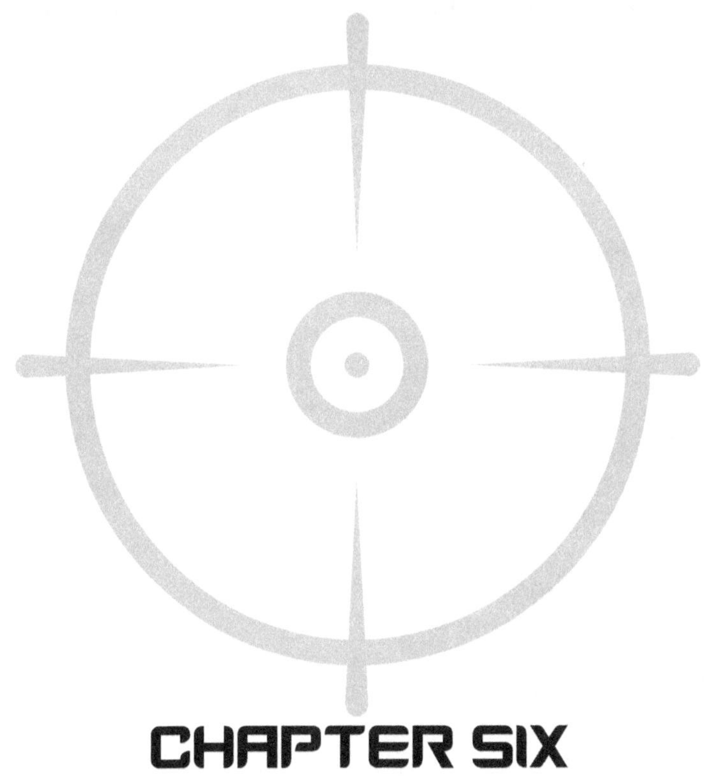

CHAPTER SIX

Admiral Mahone was on the secured telephone line talking to Captain Emacke about getting one of our submarines to the rendezvous point. She informed him it was paramount for our sub to surreptitiously slip into Chinese waters and pick up someone. At first Captain Emacke flatly refused her request that the rendezvous point was too dangerous. He was not going to risk one of his submarines for her. She insisted on her request. He was definitely emphatic. He was not going to let one of his submarines into Chinese waters. He reiterated the risk was too great.

Captain Emacke explained, "If the Chinese captured our sub, we have too much top-secret equipment in our sub for them to copy. And if captured, what do you think our Commander in Chief would think? Who orchestrated this operation? I'm sure my rank would be reduced as well as a few of your stars on your collar would be taken away. Do you get my drift?"

Admiral Mahone did not expect this negative attitude from Captain Emacke. "Captain Emacke, it is vital to our national security that we pick up this person." Admiral Mahone sat quietly holding the phone close to her ear and listened to Captain Emacke emote his personal views on the subject. She could tell he did not like women in his navy especially a woman admiral requesting one of his subs into dangerous waters. She calmly explained to the emotional captain, "that it is critical the United States extract this government official who wants to defect to our side. She explained this person will give us the edge we need to elevate our knowledge of what the Chinese are thinking. We are already behind in our national security interests and this person will add to our intelligence. This person has secret information we desperately needed."

"You'll have to clear this with Admiral Turner before I send one of my subs on this operation."

"I have already received the okay from Admiral Turner. You can give him a call if you want to." Admiral Mahone lied. She did not talk to Admiral Turner. She hoped her bluff would work. She knew Admiral Turner was on vacation for another week and could not be reached. Admiral Mahone knew being a navy admiral gave her the clout or for that matter the strong authority and powerful muscle to control obstinate subordinates.

Captain Emacke decided not to call his boss and make waves. He gave in to Admiral Mahone's request. "What are the coordinates for our sub? And when do you need one of my subs?"

Admiral Mahone supplied the information to Captain Emacke. "This will be a short task. We would need the submarine at this location tomorrow. 30.626539 degrees north and 122.064958 degrees east. The sub would be placed right next to Shanghai, China. I believe your sub would have enough movement to slowly move off the coast to pick up our guest. The depth off the coast is 17.5 meters. So, our sub could quietly slip up to the rendezvous point off the coast of Shanghai and quickly surface to pick up our guest." Admiral Mahone thanked the captain and hung up the phone.

CHAPTER SEVEN

Dusty quietly sat inside his sterile cubicle staring at the telephone for a few minutes thinking. He remembered his bank officer called to inform him that his checking account was overdrawn by $189.10 and she could transfer funds from his savings account to cover the deficit. He was appreciative she called. Also laying on his mind was the electricians who quoted him an amount of eleven thousand dollars to run a new electrical line one hundred feet from the farmhouse to the restored barn along with new wiring and lights in and around the barn. He heard one of the other analysts approach his station and say there were donuts in the kitchen. He looked up at the voice and offered a grin and a nod. Dusty glanced at the picture of Dianne and his mind heard the director say 'don't let the neighbors know of this operation. Keep the operation top secret.' However, with two inexperienced people escorting an escapee to freedom they might need a little assistance. He did not want to fail on this assignment. To cover his bases, he would have their satellite watch from above, but he needed additional security on the ground. The only person Dusty could trust would be Elliot Farnsby who works for MI6. He met Elliot in France when they both worked locating a double agent last year. Dusty headed upstairs to the satellite communications department. He wanted to call Elliot to see if he could shadow the movement in Shanghai.

Dusty waltzed upstairs into the Satellite room. He punched in the security code which would open the steel door. The room had six large television screens which two analysts were watching. He greeted both of the analysts. They both had a donut in each of their hands. The room was cold to keep the electronic equipment from overheating. To keep warm the two analysts were wearing their sweaters. Dusty handed them the coordinates for the satellite to watch Shanghai for a few days. The Hamilton Foundation had six black satellites in the sky. The analyst typed the coordinates 30.626539 degrees north and 122.064958 degrees east into the machine which would rotate the satellite circling the globe to Dusty's coordinates over Shanghai. Betty, the senior analyst, said with their new satellites which had sub-two-meter resolution, the satellites could distinguish between two adjacent objects ten feet apart and with the advanced electro- optical imagery the satellites could peer through clouds and detect someone walking on the deck of a ship in real time. Dusty picked up the satellite-phone and punched in the phone number for MI6 in London, England. The secretary answered the call and routed the call to Farnsby's office.

Dusty spoke as he looked at his watch, "Afternoon Elliot, this is Dusty Sommers."

"Morning mate. Trust you are doing fine?"

"Yes, I'm good. I need a little shadow work and I thought about you, If you have the time in the next few days?"

"What's up mate?"

"We have two inexperienced agents in Shanghai escorting someone out of Shanghai tomorrow. So, I was hoping you might watch their movement so they don't get into trouble from the Chinese security team who might be following them?"

"When would I need to be in Shanghai?"

"Tomorrow. We have Pilar flying into Shanghai from Tokyo and meeting our resident agent, Nick at the Pudong airport."

"And where would they go to meet this selected person in Shanghai?"

"To the Shanghai Porcelain shop."

"And then what happens to them?" Elliot asked as he puffed on his cigarette.

"They move to the extraction point off the coast of Shanghai."

Dusty paused and asked, "I know this is short notice. If you can't help out, maybe you might have someone who is free in Shanghai to shadow my team?"

Elliot thought for a second tapping his index finger on his desk thinking about Dusty's request. "Well cousin, this is short notice. I'm rather free now. I'm not working on any surveillance and I can take some vacation time." Elliot paused for a few seconds and replied, "Sure mate, I can help you out on this small timeline. I can fly out this evening."

"Great. Thank you, Elliot. I appreciate your help."

"Sure mate. Oh, are we playing by Moscow rules or Bangkok rules? And what might be their code to greet one another in case I might need to talk to them, so they don't feel threatened if this British person needs to help them out of a jam?"

"Pecan pie," Dusty replied. His mind remembered that Moscow rules would be too exact and too precise for this operation where thumb tacks would be placed into a wooden corner wall next to the street where the pick-up would take place which would notify the escapee in a six-hour timeframe that The game is on.

"Pecan pie. What an original password." Elliot chuckled for a moment. "Do they have a safe house in Shanghai in case they need to hide?"

"No. Nick works out of the U.S. Consulate General's office in Shanghai. There is no safe house. The two are to pick up the package and leave the same day. We would use Bangkok rules." They both understood Bangkok rules which is an offshore pickup.

"Well, if necessary, they can use our safe house in Shanghai. Bangkok rules would be most effective in this type of operation." Elliot wanted to ask Dusty who was the mystery package but decided against the question. Elliot would find out who the hot package was tomorrow. He knew he had an excellent working relationship with Dusty.

"Thanks, Elliot. I trust nothing will go wrong, but with a little insurance from you, I will feel better knowing my two agents escorting the package out of Shanghai will be safe until they reach the pickup point."

"No problem, mate. I'll stay in the background watching your chickens. Cheerio." Elliot hung up the phone. He called the travel desk for a flight to Shanghai, China.

Dusty's phone chirped. He answered the call. "Sommers here."

"I didn't mean to call you at work, but I can't get the lawn mower to work."

"Morning Dianne. Did you check to see if the lawnmower had any gasoline in it?"

Dianne replied, "Oh, maybe that is why it won't start. I wanted to mow the front yard so you won't get another citation from the township," she paused and asked, " And I was thinking instead of having the dinner party at my small apartment tomorrow night, we could have it at the farmhouse. What do you think?"

"That would be fine but we don't have a dining room table for your parents to eat on. We would have to eat in the kitchen. Your mother, I'm sure, would not be too happy eating dinner in the kitchen."

"Oh, I saw a furniture restoration shop on the town square. I could swing by and see if they might have a nice inexpensive dining room table. What do you think?"

"Sure, Dianne. That would be nice."

Dianne quickly injected, "That's her tough luck." She did not want to tell Dusty the next problem. "Oh, the toilet is backed up again and I can't get it to flush."

Dusty took a big gulp of air into his mouth and exhaled. "Go ahead and call a plumber. Maybe, they can fix the problem today."

Dianne supplied Dusty another headache. "Oh, the tree cutters were here this morning and they said they could cut down the two trees next to the barn for six hundred dollars. Boy, that is a lot of money just to cut down two trees."

"My gosh, this never ends." Dusty thought for a moment and said, " I'll swing by the hardware store to pick up a chainsaw this evening. I'll cut the trees down myself." Dusty remarked in a solid tone. "I'm not paying six hundred dollars to those thieves."

Dianne did not want to add to the mounting problems but commented, "Ya know, we need to think about getting some white paint for the farmhouse. As it looks now, it sure is an eyesore. We could get some red paint for the barn, too. I sure would like to have it looking somewhat nice for my parents when they come over tomorrow night. What do you think?"

"Yeah. I can get a couple of gallons of white house paint when I pick up the chainsaw at the hardware store this evening." Dusty thought to himself, maybe I should have purchased the farmhouse which was made of brick instead of wood. Dusty said, "Is that all? 'cause, I got to go."

"That's about it. See you tonight. Love you. Oh, one more thing. Aren't we tired of eating with those plastic forks and knives?"

"Yeah. Why?"

Dianne supplied the answer, "While at the restoration shop, I'll see if they have any nice silverware for us. All right?" "Sounds good. I have to go."

"All right. Love you. Bye."

"Love you right back, Dianne." Dusty hung up the phone and concentrated on his job.

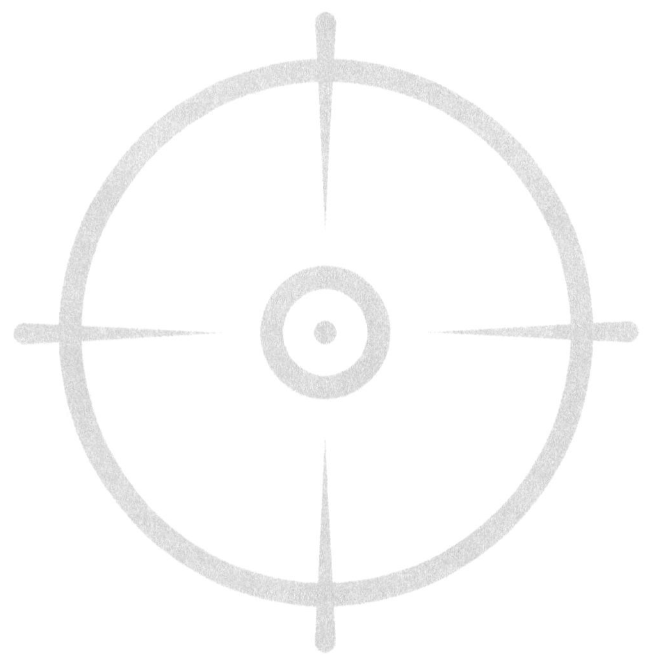

CHAPTER EIGHT

usty did not expect all these numerous problems at his farmhouse. He knew in time these headaches would slowly disappear. What was disappearing was the money from his checking account. His two credit cards were close to being maxed out. Fortunately, Dianne was supplying some of her funds toward the estate. If her mother found out her daughter was paying for some of the needs of the farm, she would hit the ceiling. Her mother did not like Dusty. Her mother thought of Dusty as a janitor, someone who cleans up accounts. Her father, who is a businessperson, in the steel beam supports for buildings looked up the Hamilton Foundation in the Dun and Bradstreet Credit Report. There wasn't much information only that they paid their bills on time listing the names of the management personnel and noting the foundation was a research company. Her father suspected the Hamilton Foundation was a front for the Central Intelligence Agency, for that matter, the Alexander Hamilton Foundation changed its name from the United American Communications Service Systems Company which supplied a vital need for security to United States. He noticed the Hamilton Foundation had no tax number as all businesses have a tax number, which clued him in the Foundation was a front for the government. He never asked Dusty what he did for the Foundation. He realized Dusty had a doctorate degree in economics from The University of Pennsylvania. He enjoyed Dusty's tenacity at the restoration of the farm.

At 36 years old, Dusty enjoyed his life especially with Dianne. She gave him purpose. He had mounting pressures at work and at the farm but his mental capacity was solid as a rock. Dusty was clean shaven standing six foot tall. He at times needed his glasses to read. Having a strong deep sounding voice, people felt secure around his presence. His smile would disarm any angry person into a tender lamb. His charismatic voice and solid stance gave the other person confidence that they could trust his word. Dusty was a person you could count on if you were in trouble. In his youth he was a cub scout who earned the three badges: the wolf, the bear and the tiger. At this early age, he was proud of his accomplishments. One time during his college days he offered to help jump start an unknown person's car battery which was dead at the grocery store's parking lot in the pouring rain. Any other person would have walked away. He opened the lady's hood and opened his truck's hood to place the jumper cables to each battery terminal. He got the lady's car started. The lady could not believe a person would help her in the pouring rain. She offered a few dollars for his help, but Dusty refused. He liked polishing his Wenjun oxblood leather soled loafers along with wearing his button-down collars on his heavily starched long-sleeved shirts. He liked to roll his sleeves up to his elbows during the day to show he was a guy who worked hard during the day. Usually, he would have a yellow number 2 pencil in his hand. And if he was stuck on a problem, he would place the pencil in between his teeth and bite down on the pencil while he figured out a solution.

Dusty earned his master's degree from the University of Indiana. One of Dusty's professors suggested that he apply to the CIA for employment. After the three-day interview at the agency, the Central Intelligence Agency hired him. At the agency he was an analyst reviewing case studies from various overseas operations looking for discrepancies. Reviewing the weekly station chiefs' reports from the numerous cities in

Europe, Dusty looked for inconsistencies in weekly to monthly secret five-page reports. Shifting though one station chief's weekly report, Dusty noticed a swing in the Riga, Latvia chief's correspondence. He spotted a traitor. Someone who was a double agent. Dusty was told to forget what he read and keep his mouth shut. His electricity and his zeal working for the agency had expired. After six years of employment, it was time to leave. He had an ax to grind. In the polygraph interview process, the agency was fixated on questions on one's sexuality. Dusty commented on their interview platform and stated why is it the need to know of one's sexuality, but rather focus on one's religion to see if the possible employee had a moral conscious, which the agency would learn if someone was a mole trying to enter their sanctuary? Also, he argued to review one's bank deposits to discover the possibility of bribes slowly becoming a double agent. He had enough of their infighting and incompetence.

He often said there were more good people going to the wall while the incompetents and alcoholics were promoted. Dusty talked to the director, who was an admiral, and explained the need for more changes. Dusty was soon ushered out and from the seventh floor. At this point he understood things were not going to change and it was time to move on. Dusty quit the agency. He was tired of their ineptness and lack of integrity. He was accepted at the University of Pennsylvania to study economics. After seven long years of teaching undergraduates economics and working tirelessly on his dissertation, Dusty earned his doctorate in economics. His three-hundred-page dissertation was titled: The Pragmatics of Caesar to Descartes to Marcuse in Understanding Price Theory Leading to Capitalism. After he earned his Ph.D., Dusty was offered prominent teaching positions at U.C.L.A., Stanford, University of Vanderbilt and M.I.T. He declined all teaching positions to be selected to work for the Alexander Hamilton Foundation. The Foundation was a research firm who also performed covert overseas operations that other agencies could not successfully gain traction. He knew the other agencies did not have the strength to perform risky operations; therefore, the Alexander Hamilton Foundation would carry forth these needed dangerous assignments. The Foundation had the bite and the muscle to move forward on any operation the other agencies could not perform. Dusty knew the other intelligence agencies were possibly riddled with double agents. To Dusty's mind, these Washington intelligence agencies lost their reliability to America. Most of their directors were a weak public figures. Dusty was fed up with the bureaucracy at the number one intelligence agency and it was time to leave. The Hamilton Foundation found their diamond in the rough in Dusty's intelligence. He was offered a salary of $120,000.00 a year. Dusty did not want an office to work in, but a cubicle would be fine with a comfortable chair. He did not have a secretary, but numerous competent people with integrity he could trust.

Occoquan looks odd and sounds odd. The native American Indians were living along the Occoquan River located what is now called the state of Virginia. The Doeg Indians settled in the area. The colonists found the Indians living along the river in 1608. The small village became a city with about one thousand inhabitants, which is now about twenty miles south of Washington, D.C. After work Dusty cruised down I-95 toward the city of Occoquan. He was to pick up two-gallon cans of white water-based house paint along with several paint brushes and a new chainsaw accompanied with an empty one-gallon plastic gas can. Dusty could not believe the merchant sold chainsaws for over one thousand dollars. He selected a chainsaw for two hundred dollars. The merchant handed Dusty a pair of plastic goggles for free. He loaded the paint cans, chainsaw and gas can into the back of his truck and strolled a few blocks down to the local jewelers on Mill Street picking up the one carat ring for Dianne. He was going to ask Dianne to marry him. Dusty fired up his Chevy truck and headed to the farmhouse which was ten minutes away. As he backed-away from the parking slot his truck back-fired, which sounded like a gunshot. A few people who strolled on the sidewalk quickly looked at Dusty's truck and then turned their heads away. Dusty grinned remembering another foolish prank he pulled on his neighbor when he was a senior in high school. He forced one of his mom's baking potatoes into the exhaust pipe of their neighbors car. Dusty watched as the gentleman started up the engine and waited for the explosion. The potato lodged in the tailpipe blocked the expelling gas exhaust from exiting, which built up a powerful back pressure force in the muffler. Dusty grit his teeth sitting in the dark bushes waiting for the explosion. Suddenly, the potato was fired out of the tailpipe rocketing across the street toward the neighbor's plate glass front window. Dusty thought the blocked tailpipe would blow out the man's muffler but the potato smashed into the plate- glass front window shattering it into tiny fragments. Dusty laughed at the incident as he grabbed his sides because he was laughing so hard. He saw lights flick on in the living room of the house across the street. Dusty was rolling on the ground chuckling. He could not believe the potato had the velocity and trajectory to travel thirty yards across the street and plow into the neighbor's living room glass window. No one knew how the plate glass shattered. Dusty chucked to himself as he cruised down Mill Street toward his farmhouse listening to jazz.

As Dusty pulled into the driveway of his farmhouse he saw Dianne's Chevy parked close to the house. He noticed the front lawn was mowed. He was pleased with Dianne's accomplishment. She did a superb job of mowing the overgrown lawn. Dusty hated mowing the grass. As he turned the truck engine off, he sat retracing the movements of his extraction assignment.

Dusty was pleased with his contacting Admiral Mahone and her selection of Lieutenant Commander Pilar Marshall on a short notice to meet Ming-Li in Shanghai. Though Pilar was new to the undercover format, Dusty believed she had the fortitude for the task. Fortunately, Nick McMasters was available to meet Pilar at the Shanghai airport and shuttle her to the pick-up point at the porcelain factory. He trusted Admiral Mahone to contact the available submarine to rendezvous at the correct latitude and longitude point off the shores of Shanghai. Dusty believed that letting Elliot Farnsby of MI6 to only shadow the extraction team so they would have a little backup in case they might run into trouble on the escape route to the submarine was the right thing to do. Dusty remembered the director saying there are only several kinds of people in the spy calculus: the dumb and the stupid. The dumb simply don't think. They are the non-achievers. They do just enough to get by. The stupid tend to hide when the assignment becomes too tough. The stupid make mistakes relying on others to do their work for them and then take the credit for the successful results. Dusty was neither dumb nor stupid. Upper management recognized Dusty as a pragmatist. Someone who can get the job done and not boast about the accomplishment. Dusty was not too worried about Pilar or

Nick, but uneasy about the rendezvous point the U.S. Navy was to provide. Hopefully, Elliot would provide some type of cover in case the Chinese police intervened in the escape. If the assignment goes south, the Chinese Government will blame the agency for the entanglement. The press would attack the agency for the foul-up. Newspapers across the United States would print about the botched escape on their front pages. The Foundation would be in the spotlight. The U.S. Congress would be in an uproar. The British would be laughing at the United States' screw up. The frogs would really distrust the Americans. The Chinese ambassador at the United Nations would lamb bast the U.S. Ambassador. The relationship between the Americans and the Chinese would be at the heated crossroads. Dusty was well aware of the possibility that things could spin out of control if his team failed to get Ming-Li safely out of Shanghai.

Dusty did not tell Dianne what exactly he did at the Hamilton Foundation only that he was an accountant at the Foundation. Dusty knew Dianne came from a wealthy family which had a horse farm. She had three horses named: Brice, Questor and Legion, which she taught them how to jump the hurdles. She came in second place with Brice in the national equestrian contest in Las Vegas when she was a junior at college. Dusty would have to tell Dianne at some point what he did for a living. After listening to Jerry Rafferty's song, *Baker Street*, Dusty turned the truck radio off and exited his truck. He slowly opened the recently painted front door. He liked the color of black on the front door. He headed into his kitchen where he saw Dianne was preparing the evening meal. He handed her a small black velvet box. He watched as Dianne reached out to receive the tiny box. Dusty grinned as he saw Dianne open the box. He saw her eyes open wide as her tears began to flood from her eyes and gently run down her cheeks. "Will you marry me?"

"Of course, I will. I love you." Dianne grabbed hold of the ring and gently placed the one carat ring onto her left hand's finger. "It looks nice sitting on my finger, like it belongs there." Dianne looked up at Dusty and kissed him. She set the velvet box on the kitchen table.

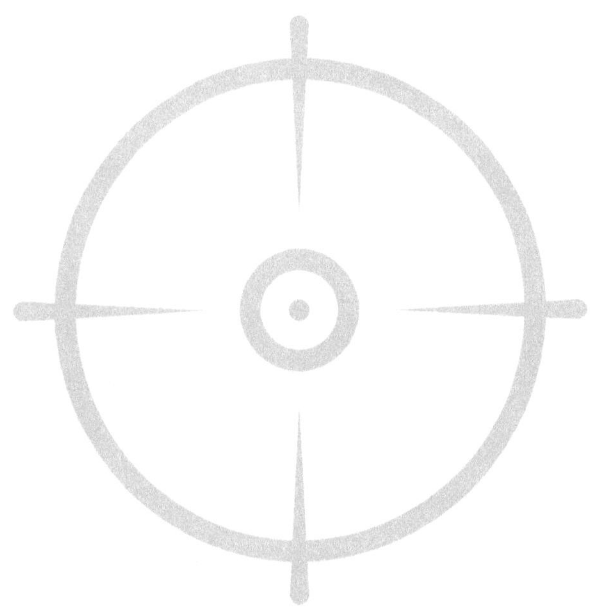

CHAPTER NINE

The mid-morning sunny day unfolded as Pilar landed at Pudong International Airport in Shanghai, China. Her flight from Tokyo was uneventful. She breezed through Chinese customs informing the Chinese official she was a tourist. Her passport was stamped and she moved searching inside the airport terminal to locate Nick.

Nick quickly recognized Pilar as she was wearing a colorful scarf. He greeted her with the password, "Pie."

Pilar responded with a serious face, "Pecan." She returned a friendly smile. She noticed his handsome face and his facial scar.

"Welcome to Shanghai. Trust your flight was good?"

"Yes, it was."

Nick said, "Let's move out of here and get a taxi. Oh, you'll be meeting my girlfriend, Candace, and her friend, Margaret. They are not part of our cover. Candace will help us get to where we are going. Then, they will depart and go on their way to the market."

"I see." Pilar said. "We'll need to go to the Jingdezhen Porcelain Artware Factory at 1176 Nanjing Xi Lu. Do you know where it is located in Shanghai?"

"No, but Candace will get us there. You don't have any luggage do you?"

Pilar looked at Nick and said, "No. Just this handbag."

Pilar and Nick walked out toward the waiting taxi area where Candace and Margaret were standing waiting for Nick and his friend. Nick said, "Let me introduce you to my girlfriend, Candace and this is her best friend, Margaret."

Pilar smiled and shook hands with Candace and Margaret. "Nice to meet you both."

Candace asked, "Where do we need to get you to?"

"The Porcelain Factory on 1176 Nanjing Xi Lu road. It is the Jingdezhen Porcelain Artware Factory. I understand it is the best place to buy porcelain artwork."

As they all climbed into the yellow taxi, Candace told the driver in Mandarin where they all wanted to go. The porcelain factory is next to Chang Jiang.

Margaret turned to Candace and said in Mandarin, "*His friend is pretty. Lookslike you might have some competition.*"

Candace glared at Margaret and replied, "*Please.*" She turned her eyes away from Margaret to watch the road. She wondered what Pilar was doing in Shanghai. Candace looked at Nick. She saw him watching the road ahead.

Pilar sat in the front seat and inquired about all the people walking about Shanghai. "I think your city is larger than New York City?" She turned to Candace.

"Yes, we have about twenty-two million people here. Are you just in Shanghai for the day?"

"Yes. I thought I'd purchase a tea pot and cups from the famous Porcelain Factory."

"Where do you work at Pilar?"

"I work out of Tokyo at the U.S. Embassy. I process visas and passports."

"How long have you known Nick?" Candace was probing. Maybe Pilar was a threat or maybe she wasn't a threat.

Quickly, Pilar had to come up with a plausible answer. "Oh, for about a year. Mostly, we talk via email and I had some vacation coming, so I decided to fly to Shanghai for the day and finally meet Nick."

Margaret said under her breath, *"How nice."* She turned her squinting eyes aiming at Candace. *"I wonder when your boyfriend is flying to Tokyo to meet her. She must look attractive coming out of the shower with all those curves?"*

"That's enough." Candace barked as she leaned forward and replied continuing her glare at Margaret, who was sitting on the other side of the taxi. Nick sat in between Candace and Margaret. He had no clue what they said in Mandarin but Pilar understood every word since she speaks fluent Mandarin where she learned the language at the University of Hawaii. Candace turned to Nick, "Aren't you glad we came along to guide you to the Porcelain Factory? If we did not come along, I know you would have gotten lost." Candace patted Nick on his shoulder and grinned.

"My, your city has a lot of smog." Pilar commented. She was going to keep silent not letting on she knew the Mandarin language. She glanced back at Candace and asked, "Could we stop and get some coffee, somewhere?"

Candace nodded and asked the taxi driver to pull into the next coffee shop.

They all exited the taxi and walked into the coffee shop. Pilar was about to ask the attendant for a cup of coffee in Mandarin but caught herself and kept her secret as she looked to Candace for help in asking for a cup of coffee. Candace ordered four cups of coffee. Candace paid for the coffee.

Pilar walked out of the coffee shop with Nick and as she sipped her hot coffee standing next to the taxi, she noticed this guy about 20 to 30 feet away wearing a blue baseball cap and sunglasses looking at them. She saw him look away. Pilar remembered this same guy from the airport. As Candace and Margaret ordered their coffee, Pilar asked Nick, "Do you see that guy," Pilar subtly pointed, "Over there with the baseball hat?"

"Yeah, why?" Nick did not turn his head but rotated his eyes to the guy and bowed his head to sip his coffee.

"I don't want to alarm you but I think this guy is following us. I wonder why he is following us? No one knows about our assignment. What are the odds this guy from the airport would catch up with us?"

Nick looked at Pilar. "I did not tell anyone." Nick took a sip of his hot coffee and asked, "Maybe our controller did?"

"Hopefully, not." Pilar turned away from Nick and focused her eyes with a satisfying grin as she saw Candace and Margaret walk toward them with their paper cups of coffee. "This coffee tastes good, doesn't it?"

They both nodded yes. As Pilar entered the front seat of the taxi, she slowly glanced back to see if the man wearing the baseball cap was continuing to watch them. She did not see him. He disappeared. Pilar looked across the street. The watcher had vanished. Pilar's radar was up. She was sure someone was watching them.

"So Pilar, what type of porcelain art piece are you looking to buy," asked Candace.

"Oh, a nice tea set with four or six teacups." remarked Pilar. It was only a 15- minute ride via their taxicab, when Pilar inquired, "Is that the porcelain store up ahead of us?"

Candace tapped the driver on his shoulder. "This is the place."

As Pilar exited the cab, she wondered how she was going to explain to Nick's girlfriend and Margaret their meeting this new person and transporting her to the rendezvous point. She wanted to grab Nick and ask when his girlfriend and Margaret would depart. Outside on the sidewalk, Pilar stood looking through the store window at numerous porcelain art pieces. She saw Candace and Margaret enter the store. Quickly, Pilar grabbed Nick's arm saying, "When is your girlfriend and Margaret leaving us? This is the place where we meet Ming-Li."

"Yes. I understand, Pilar. I'll suggest that they leave for the market from here and that maybe, you might want to see some tourist sights after words."

Pilar commented, "Fine. By the way, Nick, our guest Ming-Li will be wearing a colorful scarf." She looked to the entrance of the porcelain shop and asked, " Shall we go into the store?" Pilar looked around the store and immediately spotted Ming-Li. "Nick," Pilar tapped him on his arm and pointed. "There she is. See her with the colorful scarf?"

Nick turned his sight away from Candace and Margaret who were twenty feet away staring at some fine porcelain plates. He saw Ming-Li standing next to a store employee. "How is she going to recognize us? Is there a code word?"

"Yes. I will say red, white and blue. That is the code word." Pilar approached Ming-Li. Pilar stood across from Ming-Li and offered a small smile. Nick stood next to Pilar. Pilar softly said the code words, "Red, white and blue."

Ming-Li slightly nodded her head at Pilar. She watched Pilar extend her hand. Ming-Li looked down at Pilar's hand as she distribute three fingers. Ming-Li raised her eyes to look at Pilar's face. Ming-Li slowly raised her arm and offered to show Pilar two fingers. Then Ming-Li retracted her fingers making a fist. She waited for a moment with her eyes glued to Pilar's hand. She watched as Pilar offered five fingers from her hand. Ming-Li knew it was safe to proceed. " Are we ready to go?"

Pilar said, "Good afternoon, Ming-Li. My name is Pilar and this gentleman is named Nick. We will guide you out of Shanghai. Yes, we are ready to go."

Ming-Li said, "Next to me is my mother, Yuan. She is going with me."

"We are only instructed to take you to the rendezvous point." Pilar glanced outside. She saw the man with the ball cap and sunglasses watching them. Stinging acid filled the walls of her stomach and then the acid slowly disappeared. Pilar knew she was right. They were being followed. "Nick," She pointed toward the store's glass picture window. "See the man with the baseball cap?"

Nick scanned his eyes toward the glass window. He saw the man with the baseball cap. Nick strongly asked Pilar, "Do you want me to confront him?"

Pilar looked back at Nick, "He might be Chinese secret security watching Ming- Li. No, but we need to have your girlfriend and Margaret move on. I don't want them involved with this assignment." She turned to ask Ming-Li. "Does anyone know you would be here, today?"

"No one." Ming-Li replied confidently. "No one." She hesitated and asked, "Is there a problem?"

"Hopefully, not Ming-Li." Pilar turned to Nick saying, "Nick, can you tell your girlfriend and Margaret that we are leaving to do a tourist thing with this nice lady who offered to guide us? They can depart on their own toward the market. I can tell them it was nice to meet them and we can leave."

Nick nodded and walked toward his girlfriend and Margaret who were gazing at some fine porcelain dishes. He said they are leaving and going to do a tour of the city before Pilar has to depart on her flight.

"We'll go with you, Nick." Candace looked over to Pilar and waved.

"You can't," barked Nick.

"What do you mean, we can't?" Candace asked in a deep tone.

"Don't you and Margaret have to go to the market before it gets too crowded? We met this nice lady while Pilar was looking at some artwork and she offered to guide us to several tourist points in Shanghai."

"We can go later to the market. I want to make sure your friend doesn't get lost in Shanghai. I'm sticking to you like glue. Got it...," Candace paused looking into Nick's eyes, "Mister!" Candace grinned as she grabbed hold of one of his arms ensuring Nick, she meant what she said. Candace looked toward Pilar. "I see she has selected a teapot. Let's go see what she is going to buy?" Candace held on to Nick's arm and pulled him toward Pilar. "Have you picked out a teapot?" Candace with a pleasing face saw the teapot Pilar chose. "I like the colorful flowers and butterflies on the teapot."

"Yes. Instead of carrying this on the plane. I wonder if they can ship it to me?"

"I'm sure they can." Candace pointed to the cashier. "If you need some help explaining to the cashier that you wish to ship the teapot, let me know. I want to look at some of their other fine teacups."

"Great. Thanks Candace." Pilar walked over to the cashier and asked to have the teapot and cups shipped to her Mother and Father in Hanford, California. The cashier understood Pilar. She watched as Nick approached her at the counter.

Pilar looked outside to see if the watcher was watching them. She did not see him. Maybe he left or maybe he is waiting for them to make a move. "Nick, can you peek outside and see if the guy is looking our way?" Pilar saw Nick nod his head and walk toward the store entrance. She watched Nick poke his head around the corner of the store.

Nick looked back and saw the cashier take Pilar's teapot and teacups to the back room to be wrapped for shipping. "Pilar, I watched as the guy with the ballcap slip into a taxi. I saw him turn around and look toward us. I guess he is waiting for us to depart. What should we do?"

"Good question, Nick." Pilar thought for a moment as she looked outside and then at Nick. "First of all, we need to ditch your girlfriend and her friend."

Nick responded, "That might be a little tough."

Pilar quickly answered, "Why?"

"She wants to make sure you get back to the airport."

Pilar asked, "She doesn't know that you work undercover, right?"

"Correct. Candace doesn't know. She only knows I work for the Consulate General."

"She is going to guess what is going on with Ming-Li and you might as well tell her what we are going to do. The only wild card is her friend Margaret. Would she run to the police about what we are going to do?"

Nick asked, "So, how is Ming-Li getting out of Shanghai?"

Pilar looked around the store for wandering ears and softly said, "By submarine offshore."

"So, I guess her mother is going along, too?"

"Yep." Pilar hesitated and spoke, "I did not expect Ming-Li to bring her mother, too. Anyway, we would need to get away from the baseball guy watching us. Got any ideas?"

Nick responded, "Hey, this is the first time I have done this type of undercover work. The only other type of undercover work is for me to watch and record how many trucks deliver shipments to the docks and try to get the names of the ocean freighters. I'm stumped. Have you ever done something like this before?"

"No. I'm a Lieutenant Commander in the navy. They needed someone who could blend into the Pacific Asian culture. Being born in Thailand, I fit their requirement, so I volunteered for this assignment."

Nick was somewhat astonished that Pilar was in the navy. "No kidding. You are in the navy and you are doing this? Wow."

"Nick, make sure you keep this information which I told you a secret. All right?"

Nick nodded his head yes. "Of course, Pilar. I'll keep it a secret."

Pilar thought out loud. "How about this idea, Nick. We go out through the store's back door and hail a taxi from the other side of this store? By the way Nick, you are going to have to tell your girlfriend that we can get to the airport by ourselves. Can you do that?" Pilar gazed at Nick hoping for his agreement.

"I'll try." Nick commented as he looked over to his girlfriend and Margaret standing and looking at some porcelain cups. Nick walked over to Candace. "Candace, we are going to leave now. You and Margaret can travel on to the market." Nick glanced at Ming-Li and back to Candace and watched Margaret walk away to look at some more porcelain tea settings. "Ming-Li has offered to take Pilar and myself to several tourist places and then to the airport. All right?"

Candace listened to her boyfriend's request and watched Pilar walk over to Ming-Li viewing some more porcelain tea pots. Candace shook her head and said, "No. We can show Pilar some tourist places and we can take her to the airport."

Nick took hold of Candace's arm and said, "Candace, I have something important to tell you and I'm asking you to remain calm."

Candace squinted one of her eyes at Nick. "What are you talking about?"

Nick continued, "We are here to get Ming-Li out of the country. Presently, we have some unknown person watching us."

"What?" Candace answered in disbelief and asked, "Are you serious?"

"Yes. Very serious."

Candace asked, "So, you are taking her to the airport?"

"No."

"So how are you getting her out of the country? By train down to Hong Kong?"

"No."

"Then how?" Candace asked in a firm tone.

"You have to keep this a secret. All right?" Nick whispered into her ear. "By submarine."

Candace pulled away from Nick and chuckled with a grin. "You are pulling my leg, right?"

Nick slowly shook his head back and forth and said, "No, we are not."

Candace saw a serious side of Nick. "I don't believe you. What? You work for the Central Intelligence Agency?"

"Something like that." Nick did not smile. His eyes were like glue watching Candace's reaction.

"You're serious, aren't you?"

"That is why Pilar and I," he paused, "are asking that you and Margaret leave us, so you can go to the market."

"So, Pilar is an undercover agent?"?

"Something like that. Just for the day to assist Ming-Li out of the country."

"How interesting. I understand you, but all the more, you might need me to help you navigate through the city, if you are telling me the truth?"

"Yes, Candace. I am telling you the truth."

"How is it that you did not tell me you are working for the CIA."

"I do not work for the CIA?"

"Then who do you work for?"

"The Consulate General. Candace," Nick paused and took hold of her arm. "You need to keep this quiet and do not tell Margaret. She has to be kept in the dark, all right? She cannot be involved with this."

"Yes, yes, yes." Candace stated. "I don't believe this. I've been sleeping with a spy."

"No Candace. I am not a spy."

"My gosh. If we get caught, then it is prison time for us. Oh, my gosh." Candace was silent for a moment. She started to become very nervous. Her eyes looked left and then to the right. "Are you carrying guns?"

Nick started to sense Candace was getting tense. "No. We do not carry guns.

Can you handle all this, Candace?"

"I guess so." Candace paused to catch her breath. She placed her hand on Nick's shoulder. "This is too much reality for me."

Nick answered, "That is why we need you and Margaret to go to the market to get away from us."

"I understand what you are saying, but you don't know the city like I do. You and Pilar would get lost."

"Yes, Candace. I understand what you are saying. I think it is best if you travel to the market to get away from our assignment. Besides, Pilar has caught someone possibly following us."

Candace felt uneasy. She grabbed Nick and hugged him. "I love you. I'm all right, now. It is just a little shocking what you just told me. It threw me for a moment. No, Nick. I'll stay with you and Pilar getting Ming-Li to a safe place. I'll keep Margaret in the dark. All Right?" Candace blinked her eyes several times as she realized what Nick said and asked, "What? Someone is following us?"

"It is a possibility. Okay. I believe we need to leave this place through the back door, since someone might be following us." Nick motioned to Pilar and pointed to the back door. He saw her nod, yes. He watched Pilar walk over to Ming-Li and her mother and tell Ming-Li we were leaving though the back door.

Margaret was puzzled as she watched Pilar and Nick head toward the back door of the porcelain shop. She asked Candace, "Why are we leaving by the back door? Shouldn't we go out the front door and get a taxi? Why are we doing this?"

Candace quickly told her friend, "My old boyfriend is following us. I need to get away from him. This is why we are leaving by the back door. Understand, now?"

"Okay. I get it. Does Nick know about your old boyfriend following us?" Margaret strolled toward the rear exit.

Candace responded, "Yes, I just told him. I don't want them to have a confrontation that is why we are leaving through the back door. All right?"

Nick looked left and then right while they all stood outside behind the building.

"Which way do we go?" The ally was clear. Only a stray dog looked at them.

Pilar took charge. "Let's go to our right and grab a taxi and head away." She glanced down the busy street and looked at Nick's worried face. She could tell he was in deep water by the way he kept looking around back and forth for the guy who was watching them.

Nick said, "I'm hungry. You know I could handle a couple of tacos."

Candace commented, "You are always hungry. By the way, what are taycos?"

"Tacos are a Mexican meal. The outer shell is a hard corn or a soft flour shell which both shells are held in the palm of your hand. Inside the shell you fill it with cooked beef, chicken or pork with cheese and you can add beans, lettuce, onions and cut up tomatoes. I have yet to see a taco- stand in Shanghai."

On the busy street ahead of them sat an empty cab. Candace pointed to the waiting taxicab. They all crossed the street safely. "I'm sure we all can fit into one cab. It will be a little crowed." Candace opened the front door for Ming-Li and her mother to sit together in the front seat and then opened the back door of the cab for Nick, Pilar and Margaret to sit in the back seat. "Nick, sit next to the window behind the taxi driver and I can sit on your lap. She watched Pilar sit next to the other passenger rear window as Margaret sat in the middle seat. Candace instructed the cab driver to drive straight ahead and at the light take a right, back toward the airport. She looked at Pilar. "Is this way all right?"

Pilar said, "For now, yes." She looked back through the rear dirty cigarette- filled window of the cab to see if the watcher saw them. She felt the forward motion of the cab slowly push her back into her black vinyl seat. For a moment, she thought this assignment was going to be a breeze, but now wondered about this task. She missed talking to her husband, Captain Chester Marshall. She wished she could have a warm hug from him about now.

The taxi driver picked up speed on the highway. All of a sudden the taxi started to swerve to the right at 60 MPH. The driver corrected his steering as he slowed down to the side of the highway. The taxi stopped and the driver got out. They saw him walk around to the right side of the taxi looking at the flat tire. The driver shook his head and walked to open the trunk. He pulled out the jack and spare tire. Candace and Pilar could see the spare tire was nearly bald without much tread.

Pilar said, "Let's get out and see if we can grab another taxi." Pilar noticed another taxi had stopped and parked about one hundred yards behind them. She knew it was the watcher. She pulled Nick away from everyone else and asked, "Aren't you a lieutenant junior grade in the navy?"

"Yes, but I'm not to tell anyone that information."

"By the way, Nick," Pilar kept her sight looking forward and continued, "slowly look behind us and I believe it is the watcher sitting in the waiting taxi. Don't stare but casually look behind me."

Unexpectedly, another taxi slowly pulled in front of them and stopped.

Candace asked in Mandarin if they could get a lift? She saw the driver motion yes. Candace walked over to Pilar and whispered, "Why is there another taxi parked behind us?"

Pilar gazed at Candace. "That is probably the guy who is watching us."

"What is our next move?"

Margaret noticed the parked taxi behind them. She turned to Candace and asked, "Is that your boyfriend in the parked taxi?" She watched as she saw Candace nod her head, yes.

Candace quickly said to Margaret, "Don't stare at the taxi. Just look away."

Pilar thought to herself, if we could get away from here, we might lose the watcher. Where could we hide? At the Consulate General offices? Someone would be asking too many questions. Pilar turned to Candace as they walked to the waiting taxi. "Candace, we need to hide someplace for a while and get away from the guy who is following us and not at Nick's Consulate General offices. Got any ideas?"

"Yeah. How about where I work? It is a huge warehouse. We could go in the back way and there is an office where we can be unnoticed. But first, I'll tell the driver to go to the Shanghai market. The market is only a ten-minute drive from here. We can get some food there." Candace pulled Pilar's arm and quietly said, "Nick told me about getting Ming-Li out of Shanghai. Your secret is safe with me."

"Great idea, Candace. Maybe we can duck out the back way of the market and lose this guy watching us. Let's not tell your friend Margaret what we are doing, all right?"

"I told her the guy watching us is my x-boyfriend." Candace opened the door to the taxi. She sat on Nick's lap.

"That was pretty smart of you, Candace."

Margaret turned to Candace asking, "What was smart of you?"

"Oh, to go to the market to get some food. To get Mr. hungry, happy." Candace nudged Nick and grinned.

While Pilar's eyes boar a hole into the numbing highway ahead, her mind strayed. She longed to hear Chester's soothing voice. She missed her bedroom backrubs from his strong hands massaging her neck and back muscles. Pilar loved her navy captain's tender kisses especially with her legs wrapped around his legs. For a moment, her eyes slowly closed. She could hear Chester calling her by her nickname, 'well, my dolphin,' given to her by her aunt from Thailand. Like a growing vine curled around a tree limb, Pilar loved her husband's hard body entangled with hers. Her fingertips touched where her diamond necklace laid on her chest. The diamond necklace which Chester gave her when he asked her to marry him was gone. She thought it would be inappropriate wearing a diamond ring on her finger in the navy but a diamond necklace would be unassuming. She gave it to Admiral Mahone for safe keeping. She heard Candace's voice which snapped her back into reality.

Candace told the taxi drive to pull over to the market. "We can get some quick food here." She looked at Pilar. "This market has fine food."

They walked into the crowded food market and they gathered around the chicken sandwich bar. The order taker spoke English so Pilar ordered a sandwich for everyone along with a soda.

Ming-Li asked Pilar, "When do we make the move to leave?"

Pilar presented a grin to calm Ming-Li. "We need to get away from this guy who is following us. We don't know who he is." She watched as Ming-Li turned her sight on eating her sandwich.

Nick approached Pilar. "I believe I saw the guy watching us. He is standing in the row behind me."

Pilar looked over to the second row behind Nick. She saw the watcher. "How about this, Nick. You slowly go around to the row where this guy is standing and I'll walk to the front of the row. You approach him and ask him who he is? Sound good?"

Nick finished his chicken sandwich. "Sounds good to me. I hope this guy doesn't have a gun."

"If he does have a gun, just back away. All right?"

"No problem, Pilar."

Pilar finished her sandwich and watched Nick walk around to the end of the row and gain ground toward the watcher. Pilar began her stroll toward the row where the watcher stood. She saw Nick talk to the watcher. Suddenly, the watcher pushed Nick back and moved forward toward Pilar. Her eyes grew larger as she saw the watcher with the blue LA baseball cap wearing sunglasses and a polo shirt and blue jeans. When he approached Pilar, he used his shoulder to ram her away from him. She tried to stop him. Pilar flew backwards. Her elbow floated to the shelf knocking down some cans of food. She was flying fast to the market floor. Pilar hit the floor hard. She tried to grab his foot, but he kicked her hand away as he darted away.

Nick ran toward her and helped Pilar from the floor. "You all right, Pilar? Did you recognize him?"

"Yes, I'm fine. Thanks for your help getting me up. I just did not expect him to knock me down. No. I have never seen him before. At least he knows we are aware of his watching us." She looked around the market trying to see which way he left. "Did you see which way he went?"

"No, I didn't."

Candace rushed over to help Pilar recover from her fall. "You okay?"

"I'm fine, Candace. Thanks for asking." Pilar motioned to Ming-Li. Let's move out of here. She turned to Candace. "Which way out of here? Preferably, the back way into the alley. Can you get us a taxi, Candace? Oh, and let's head south to the Jinshan District."

Candace was a bit startled by Pilar's Mandarin accent. "No problem. You pronounced the Jinshan District like you knew Mandarin. Do you know Mandarin?"

Pilar pulled Candace closer and whispered, "Yes. I picked it up in Hawaii. Can we keep this a secret between you and me?"

"Of course, Pilar. I'll get us a taxi." Candace exited the market and headed out to the alley. She could smell the garbage piling up along the red brick walls of the store. She questioned herself. Why am I doing this? She answered herself. Because I love Nick? Of course, I love him. Maybe, he will ask me to marry him and take me away from here. I'd love to live in America. She saw this dog sniffing around a garbage bag. She concentrated on getting a taxi for them.

Pilar gathered Margaret, Ming-Li and her mother. She pointed to follow Candace.

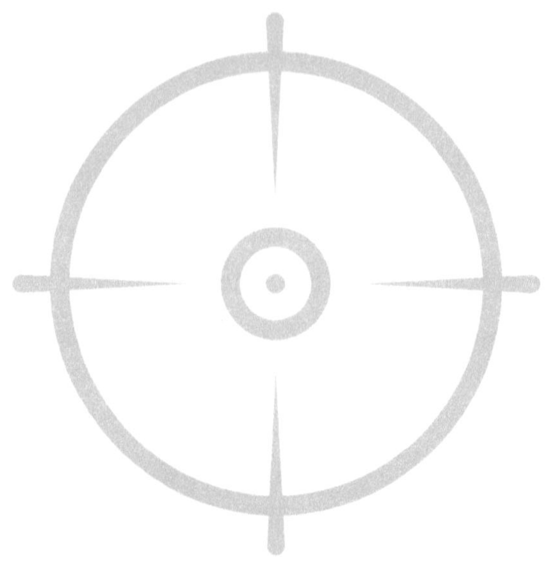

CHAPTER TEN

Director Laube received a call from one of his counter parts at MI6 informing him of a delicate matter. One of their MI6 agents was a double agent. The director said he would keep this quiet. He asked, "Where is the agent now ?"

Barry Nightingale said, "We have been watching him for the past year at the circus. It is confirmed. He is our fox in the hen house. Elliot Farnsby is our double agent and he has flown to Shanghai, China. Watch your back."

Director Laube thanked Barry and asked his secretary to call Dusty into his office. He watched Dusty pop into his office. "Hi Dusty, I received a call from MI6 this morning. They informed me Elliot Farnsby is a double agent and he has flown to Shanghai, China. Didn't you work with him last year with the Frogs in France?"

Dusty was stunned by the news but did not show his tense emotion to the director. He looked directly at the director with a numb face. "Yes, I worked with him in France last year." In a serious tone he said, "I could not detect he was a double agent."

"Make sure you tell our other analysts about Elliot Farnsby being a double agent. If you have any contact with him, let me know. All right?"

"Yes sir. Is that all?" Dusty's mind froze for a moment. He thought if he told the director he talked and reached Elliot to follow his team in Shanghai, the director might take him off the assignment. On the other hand, if he kept his previous call with Elliot a secret and the director found out later that Elliot was truly a double agent, Dusty would be reprimanded or fired. Dusty nodded his head. "I called Elliot to see if he could shadow the team in Shanghai."

"I see. Knowing the British as I do, they are always quite nervous about their agents turning into double agents. Quite frankly, Dusty, I think Barry Nightingale is the double agent. Anyway, if you trust Elliot from your previous experience with him, then you did the right thing to have him follow your team." The director grinned. "Don't worry too much about it, Dusty. Since our other agents are busy in Shanghai, I would have asked a fellow agent for some back up shadowing, too. I'm confident Elliot is not a double agent." As the director turned away, he moved his head back toward Dusty and said, "Keep me advised about our guest coming to America." He tapped Dusty on his shoulder and walked away.

"Yes, sir." Dusty looked at his watch. It was time to leave for the evening. He logged off his computer and locked up the paperwork into his safe.

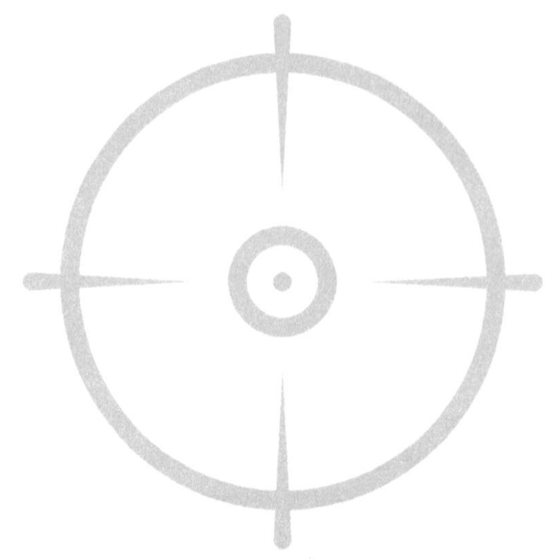

CHAPTER ELEVEN

usty pulled into the stone driveway at his farm; He quickly noticed his future in-laws had already arrived. They arrived too early as far as Dusty was concerned. As he walked next to their new black Mercedes parked in the driveway, Dusty peered into the car and saw the car had red leather seats. Dusty mouthed, "It must be nice." He raised his eyes to see the new white paint on the farmhouse. It looked good. Dianne did a fantastic job. The black paint on the farmhouse window shudders looked smart. As Dusty opened the front door, he decided he was not going to ask his future father-in-law permission to marry Dianne. Dusty knew if he did ask permission, the answer would have been a flat no. So why waste his breath on the subject? Dusty cordially greeted Dianne's parents. He watched Dianne open a $50.00 bottle of Chardonnay which her parents brought.

He extended his hand as he shook Dianne's father's hand. Dusty did not particularly like Dianne's father. He thought her father was rather too righteous. So, Dusty enjoyed by saying, "That is a nice-looking Chevrolet or is it a Lexus?"

"Oh no. It is a new Mercedes. I just picked it up two days ago."

"Sorry. I don't know one car from another. You have chosen a fine car." Dusty grinned as he looked down at his polished loafers and back toward Dianne's father. Dusty liked poking fun at his future father-in-law.

Holding his glass filled with chardonnay, Dianne's father said, "A toast to you both. May you both have happiness, wealth and good health in your years together." He raised his glass and watched as his wife, his daughter and Dusty also raised their wine glasses. "I'm happy for your both."

Dusty was surprised by his future father-in-law's toast. He watched as they all took a sip from their glasses. He glanced at Dianne's father. "Thank you for your kind thoughts for us."

Dianne's mother said, "I see my daughter is wearing a wonderful diamond ring. We are pleased you two are moving forward." She offered a positive grin. She turned to her daughter. "So, have you two set a date on the wedding?"

Dianne looked straight into her mother's eyes. "Oh, probably before Thanksgiving."

"Isn't that rather soon?"

"No. We want a small wedding."

"You have to plan your invitations and book a church and then make a reservation to have your wedding dinner at a posh hotel in New York?"

"That would be nice for you, but we want a small wedding at the farm." Dianne turned and walked toward the kitchen to check on their dinner. She heard her mother follow her into the kitchen.

Her mother was direct. "You're not pregnant are you?"

Dianne turned around to face her mother. "No mother. I am not pregnant. Do you think we could have a nice dinner?" Dianne turned around to pull the roast out of the oven. She took hold of her wine glass and finished it in one gulp. She marched out to the dining room and poured herself another glass of chardonnay.

Dusty asked her parents if they would like to take a tour of the barn?

"You two go ahead. I don't think I could walk out to the barn in these shoes. Besides, I'll help Dianne getting the dinner on the table," Dianne's mother grinned.

As his future father-in-law strolled out toward the barn with Dusty, he commented, "I just bought a 50-foot Alden yacht."

"How much did that set you back?"

"About eight hundred thousand dollars. Since I don't play golf, this was a great past time to have and I don't have to keep buying golf balls. She has two masts with a teak deck. The hull us painted black. She is a beauty. I have her moored at the Miles Yacht Club which is across from Annapolis Naval Academy. When you have the time, you and Dianne can drive over and we can go sailing for the day."

"Where have you docked the boat, again?"

"Miles Yacht Club."

"How nice. I have heard of that yacht club. I have never been there." Dusty took a sip from his glass of wine and said as they stood in front of the barn, "She needs a little work on the roof and some red paint." He glanced at Dianne's dad. "I've got a used Massey-Ferguson tractor coming tomorrow with a mower attached. I plan to buy some goats which will reduce the farm taxes."

"Sounds like you have a great plan for this acreage." Dianne's father turned and tapped Dusty on his shoulder. He took a sip from his wine glass. "Shall we return to see what the girls are doing for our dinner?"

"Sure."

"Oh, I forgot to tell you, I just purchased a company last week in Meadville, Virginia."

"What does that company do?"

"The company is called Tapco. Kind of an odd name. The previous owner drained the company of all funds. He had to sell the firm. Tapco is the leading producer of structure steel support products. They make floor jacks and steel columns for bracing. The company was up for sale. Their annual sales were over nine million the previous year, which dwindled down to $259 thousand last year as operating profit. I plan to grow this company by buying a few more companies. Their earnings before interest and taxes becomes an indicator of the company's profitability. You just take the revenue minus the expenses excluding the tax and interest earnings, which is now called EBITS. The EBIT is also called the operating earnings or operating profit before interest and taxes. I'm looking for a manager to run this company. I was thinking of you with your economics degree and accounting background. I think it would be a perfect fit. What do you think, Dusty?"

"Let me talk it over with Dianne. Where do you have her moored, again?"

"I have her moored at the Miles Yacht Club which is across from Annapolis Naval Academy. When you have the time, you and Dianne can drive over and we can go sailing."

"Sounds like a date." Dusty said to himself as he grinned, 'It must be nice.'

The future father-in-law boasted about his new purchase as he stopped and turned to Dusty. "Yeah, the yacht has two masts and a teak deck. The inside cabin, which we call a saloon, is spectacular. All beautifully varnished. The yacht has a four-cylinder Yan Mar diesel engine. The sails are all new and white. She sleeps six. He stopped and took a sip of his wine. "Dusty you and my daughter need to come and see my yacht." He looked toward the farmhouse. "I see they are calling us in for dinner."

As Dianne's father and Dusty walked into the kitchen, Dusty asked, "Maybe, we could play monopoly, later?"

Dianne quickly turned and pointed at Dusty saying, "He cheats!"

Dianne's mother asked, "What do you mean he cheats?"

Dianne looked directly at her mother. "Seriously, he cheats at monopoly."

"How does he cheat? You can't cheat at Monopoly. Everyone is in front of you as you roll the dice. Then you move the hat or race car on the board."

"First of all, he acts as the banker handing out the money for every player. He then grabs a handful of five-hundred-dollar bills and carts them off to the bathroom and hides the money. During the game when he lands at Park Place with a hotel on it, he'll go to the bathroom to collect some of his hidden money. He'll walk back to the game and pay the bill with his hidden funds. Thus, staying in the game. That is how he cheats. Get it?"

Dianne's mother looked at Dusty. "Really, Dusty?"

"I play by Richard Nixon rules." Dusty grinned and poured himself a glass of wine.

Dianne had CNN on the television. She mentioned that CNN reported the Chinese security was looking for one of their missing government officials. The phone rang. Dianne said, "Who would be calling at this hour?" Dianne answered the call. She handed the phone to Dusty. "It's for you. Don't be too long, dinner is on the table."

Dusty had the feeling it was the Hamilton Foundation calling him. He held the phone close to his ear and listened. The secretary said Admiral Mahone called and for Dusty to call her immediately. He did not have the admiral's number. The admiral's number was in his safe at the Foundation. He would have to leave the dinner party for at least an hour. He explained to Dianne and her parents. "We are working on the budget and there is a huge problem. I need to get to the office and solve the numbers problem. I need to call this admiral about the budget and the phone number is at the office."

Dianne asked, "Where is the admiral located?"

"Hawaii." Answered Dusty.

"Why don't you look the number up on the internet. I'm sure you can find the admiral's number on it instead of going to the office."

"I'll only be a minute. Please, go ahead and start dinner." Dusty walked into his small office at the farmhouse and turned on the computer. He located the naval base in Hawaii and jotted down the number. He dialed the phone number and asked for Admiral Mahone.

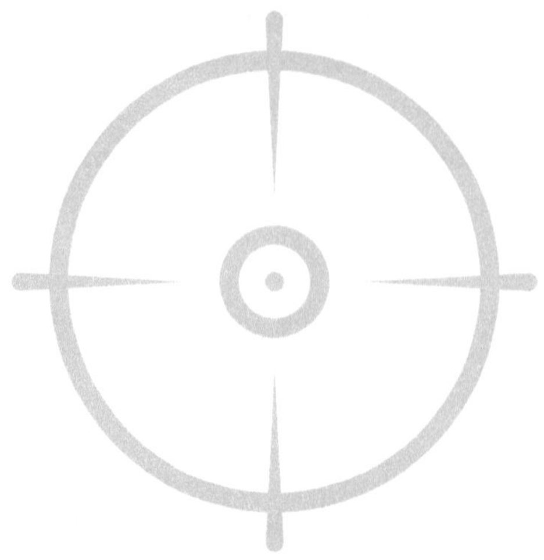

CHAPTER TWELVE

Petty Officer Clermont glanced at the wall clock. It was close to five o'clock, time to head to the enlisted club to hoist a few drinks. Just a few more weeks in the navy and he would be off to college. The telephone rang. He turned to Admiral Mahone. "Admiral, phone call from Admiral Ambrose."

"Thank you, Clermont." Admiral Mahone picked up the phone but did not sit down in her office chair. She knew Admiral Ambrose was a short-tempered feisty four-star admiral in charge of all of the submarines in the Pacific theater. He was not a graduate of Annapolis, but rather rose from an enlisted petty officer to having stars on his shoulder boards. She knew he was an accomplished man. She held the receiver close to her ear. She remembered him having a thin pencil mustache. She compared him to a wild-eyed pistol waver.

"I see you tried to commandeer one of my subs. Was it the USS Connecticut?" asked an irritated Admiral Ambrose.

"Yes, admiral."

"I'll have you busted down to a third-class petty officer. You read me, Mahone?" barked Admiral Ambrose. He never whispered.

Admiral Mahone listened to his friction.

"I have turned the USS Connecticut around and sent her on another assignment. If you want to use one of my subs, you need to ask me. Got it!"

"If you have forgotten, I have three stars on my shoulder boards and being the Deputy Operations Officer in Hawaii, I have the authority to direct any ship or any boat, which I deem necessary. And it was necessary and proper for me to direct the USS Connecticut to this particular destination to rescue someone."

"Who wanted this operation and where was the sub going?"

"That information is top secret. We needed the submarine to pick up some people off the coast of China. These people are vital to our national security."

"Off the coast of China! Are you nuts? This submarine is not a taxi service, Admiral Mahone."

"The team will be trapped. They can't fly out. The only way out is via one of our submarines. You just sealed their fate, Admiral Ambrose."

An angry Ambrose fired back in his deep voice, "I don't care."

While listening to Admiral Ambrose on his continual bark like a junk yard dog, Admiral Mahone snapped her fingers several times to get Yeoman Clermont's attention. She saw him poke his head around her office door. She slipped Clermont a phone number. Admiral Mahone held her hand over the phone's receiver and asked, "Clermont, can you call the number on this slip of paper and have Dusty call me immediately." She saw her yeoman nod yes and watched him leave her office to make the call.

"Furthermore Admiral Mahone, I'll make sure you lose your officer's rank and privileges after I talk to the Chief of Naval Operations. I'll have you removed from your duties."

At this point, Admiral Mahone knew he hated women in his navy. She detested men with a mean attitude. He wasn't a small, minded man but a little man. She wondered how he rose to the rank of admiral? She remembered Herman Wouk's book, *The Caine Mutiny*, where the phrase in the book was the navy was designed by geniuses to be run by clods. Admiral Ambrose was an idiot. She wasn't going to listen to his bark anymore. She hung up the phone by slamming the receiver down on its cradle which cut him off in midsentence. She had no time for his nonsense, people's lives were at risk. She knew he didn't even want to listen to reason. She saw Yeoman Clermont return to her office. "Did you make the call?"

"Yes, admiral. I made the call."

"Thank you. You know Clermont, Admiral Ambrose reminds me of a fly. A really annoying fly. Never become a fly, Clermont. In the heat of battle, never lose your cool, keep your calm. As you listened, Admiral Ambrose became extremely angry." The call was to Dusty. She would let him know there would be no submarine to pick up his people. Admiral Mahone sat down thinking.

"Thanks for the advice, Admiral Mahone." Clermont returned to his desk in the outer office.

"Since it is a little after five, have a nice weekend, Clermont." She realized it was up to her to find a new way for the extraction team to leave Shanghai. She knew if she didn't get the team out of China, there would be severe repercussions. The Hamilton Foundation would blame the navy for the screw-up. Admiral Mahone knew they could not get Ming-Li out of China by using the airlines since the Chinese security would be watching. She wondered if the British would have a submarine available. Having the Brits in on the top-secret operation would be risky. Someone might leak the information to their press. She was stumped on how to get the team out of Shanghai when Pilar and Nick were searching for the submarine off the coast of Shanghai. Impatiently, she waited for Dusty's call. Her navy stars were out on a limb and Admiral Ambrose was going to saw the limb off by talking to the CNO about her commandeering one of his subs for a clandestine operation off the coast of China. She could hear the first crack of the limb as it inched toward the ground. The pain of command entered her thinking.

Before Clermont left for the weekend, the telephone rang. He picked up the phone. He yelled out to Admiral Mahone, "Admiral, CNO Taylor is on the horn for you."

"Thank you, Clermont." Admiral Mahone was expecting the Chief of Naval Operations phone call. "Afternoon Admiral Taylor."

"Good evening Admiral Mahone. I'll come right to the point. I received a call from an angry Admiral Ambrose telling me you tried to commandeer the USS Connecticut. Is this right?" The Chief of Naval Operations was direct but a fair naval officer.

"Yes sir, I did," replied Admiral Mahone.

"Can you tell me your reasoning for wanting the sub?"

"The Alexander Hamilton Foundation requested that the navy assist in one of their covert operations. It was imperative we help them out. I took the initiative to comply."

"Why did they want our help?"

"Confidentially, the Hamilton Foundation wants to extract a high-ranking Chinese government official and our sub would assist in the operation."

"And where was the USS Connecticut to pick up this person?"

"Off the coast of Shanghai, China. Ming-Li who is head of their cyber operations apparently had enough of their oppressive government and wanted to defect."

"I see." The CNO paused. "You do know, if the USS Connecticut was captured by the Chinese navy, this would be a serious break in our relationship between the United States and China. I would immediately be called on the carpet by our president demanding an answer. And, of course, I would have been in the dark on this operation. If the Chinese had captured the USS Connecticut in their waters, they would have our top-secret submarine technology and they would be reviewing how our propeller operates so silently, let alone our sailors in prison. To undo this breach, we would get our sailors back but not the USS Connecticut with all of its technology. If you recall, the North Koreans still have the USS Pueblo." The CNO paused, again. In a deeper baritone voice he said, "Do you get my drift?"

"Yes sir." A compliant Admiral Mahone replied, "Admiral Taylor, we have an extraction team in Shanghai and they will be looking for our sub to pick them up. And now, the team will be searching for the sub. Admiral Ambrose did not want to listen to reason." She paused and commented, "I'm no proctologist, but I know an asshole when I hear him talk down to me." She heard Admiral Taylor chuckle a few time over the phone. "So, what do we tell the Hamilton Foundation when they ask, where is the submarine we promised to extract the team in China?" She listened for an answer.

"At this time, this is the Foundations' problem, not ours." The CNO tempered his immediate annoyance to a calm logical reason. "Who are the people in Shanghai?"

Janis answered, "We have Lieutenant J.G. Nick McMasters, who works for the U.S. Consulate Office in Shanghai and Lieutenant Commander Pilar Marshall, who is my Intelligence officer in Hawaii."

The CNO thought for a moment. "Is Pilar Marshall the wife of Captain Chester Marshall?"

"Yes, sir."

"I met her at a briefing once at the Pentagon in Washington. She was brilliant. I was impressed with her knowledge about China. How was she selected for this assignment?"

"The Hamilton Foundation requested a Pacific Asian who can blend into the Chinese culture. Since Pilar speaks fluent Mandarin, I asked her to volunteer for this assignment. She would be a perfect fit." Their conversation went silent.

Admiral Mahone pressed the phone closer to her ear. She listened to a haunting hum. She slowly inhaled and she grit her teeth. She thought, here it comes, I'm relieved from my duties.

"You didn't pressure Pilar into this assignment, did you?"

"No sir. I did not."

There was a long silence again over the receiver. "I think Captain Marshall is in Sasebo Naval Base in Japan. I believe he earned the Navy Cross for his bravery against a Chinese destroyer a couple of years ago. I don't have that medal. Nonetheless, I believe it is less than five hundred nautical miles from Sasebo to Shanghai." The CNO was going to diplomatically give Admiral Mahone an out to save his two sailors in Shanghai. He did not want any of his sailors swinging from the yardarm. "Why don't you give him a call. Maybe, he can rescue our two sailors?"

"Thank you Admiral. I shall, " remarked Admiral Mahone. She took a deep gulp of air. She was relieved the CNO listened to her.

"For what it is worth, Janis, I would have done the same thing, but notified my boss. Best of luck to you and please keep me informed." He hung up the phone.

"Aye, aye, Admiral." Admiral Mahone looked up the phone number for Sasebo Naval Base. She dialed the number. Some yeoman answered. "Good afternoon, I am looking for Captain Chester Marshall. Can you locate him for me?"

The faceless sailor answered, "Yes, ma'am. He is at the Bachelor officers' quarters. I'll ring his room."

Admiral Mahone reached Captain Marshall. She immediately explained the problem of turning-two Shanghai, China to rescue a guest. She did not tell him his wife, Pilar, would be one of the people he would also rescue. She mentioned to have a zodiac boat aboard his ship to enter the Chinese territorial waters to pick up the people and his ship was to remain outside in international waters at all times. If he could gather a few navy seals for the mission, that would be icing on the cake, advantageous. She heard him agree to the covert assignment. She was relieved he could move quickly on this mission.

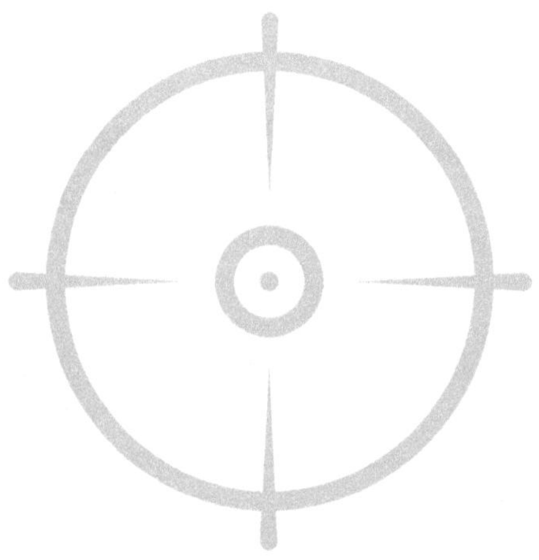

CHAPTER THIRTEEN

As soon as Captain Chester Marshall hung up the phone from Admiral Mahone, he dressed in his khaki uniform and ran from the BOQ down to the docks. The moored ships were only one hundred yards away. The first ship moored at the wooden pier was the frigate, USS Elrod. He walked up the ladder to the frigate and he saluted the ensign and asked permission to come aboard. Chester went up to the bridge to talk to the skipper of the USS Elrod, Earl Matthews. "Morning Earl. How fast can the Elrod get underway?"

"Morning Chester." Commander Matthews had a puzzled look on his face. Why was Captain Marshall here so early? "Oh. Right, now, if you wish, why?"

"I received an urgent call from Admiral Mahone who is in Hawaii. She asked if I could locate a ship and set a course to Shanghai, China."

Commander Matthews asked, "What's in Shanghai, China?"

"We need to pick up a guest as she put it. Does the Elrod have enough diesel fuel for the trip?"

"Yes, sir. The Elrod is all gassed up and ready to go."

"Great. Let's cast off."

Commander Matthews commented, "We have a skeleton crew aboard. Also, we have a few electricians working in the engine room. I think they need to check on their work to see if the electrics are working properly."

"That's fine." Chester walked over to the chart table and looked at the current map of Japan and China. "If you would, set a course to Shanghai, China. You do have a zodiac aboard, don't you, Earl?"

"Yes, sir, we do." Commander Matthews picked up the 1MC mic and said, "Prepare to get underway. Boats, single up all lines."

Chester glanced from the wheelhouse to the side of the Elrod and watched the boatswain mate pick up the bow line and toss it to the dock and then quickly walk toward the aft on the Elrod to toss the last of the hemp lines to the edge of the dock. He could feel the vibration of the diesel engines through the steel deck as the Elrod slowly pulled away from the pier. Suddenly, the electricity on the frigate died. "What happened?" He looked at Earl.

Earl barked on the 1MC to the engine room. "What happened?" He heard the engine room explain the fuse to the electric generator blew and there was a small fire which was quickly extinguished. Earl glance at Captain Marshall, "We can limp the Elrod back to its slip." He pointed to the destroyer, which was docked one hundred feet away from the Elrod. "You can take the Ingersoll. Connie Resnis is the skipper of the destroyer."

As the Elrod slowly was moored back to its slip, Chester hopped off the frigate and ran toward the destroyer. He ran up the gang plank and saluted the ensign. Permission was granted for Captain Marshall to come aboard. He climbed the ladder to the bridge to talk to the skipper of the Ingersoll. His eyes grabbed hold of the young lady with the Lieutenant Commander gold oak leaves on her collar. "Morning, commander, I am Captain Chester Marshall and the navy needs your destroyer for an important mission. Can you help me on this?"

Connie Resnis was surprised to receive Captain Marshall this early morning. She knew of him but never met him. "Morning Captain Marshall. I'm Lieutenant Commander Connie Resnis. The skipper of the Ingersoll. Yes, sir. We can help you on this assignment." She extended her hand and gave a firm handshake.

"Good to meet you Connie. Can we get underway, immediately?"

"Yes sir." Connie took hold of the 1MC and in a strong voice told the engine room to get underway. She looked over the side of the Ingersoll and saw the boatswain mate. She told him to single up the forward and aft lines. She looked at the helmsman and said, "All back, slow and when we clear the dock make the Ingersoll dance on the water to the open sea. Got it, Henry?"

The helmsman, Henry Miller, was a very competent second-class helmsman.

"Yes Commander. Flank speed ahead."

Connie asked, "Where are we going Captain?"

"Off the coast of China. To be more specific, to remain in the international waters off the coast of Shanghai. We are to pick up a guest. Do you have a zodiac aboard you ship?"

"Yes sir, we do."

Destroyer: USS Ingersoll

NavSource Naval History

Photographic History of the United States Navy as a U.S. government publication, is in the public domain..

The destroyer, USS Ingersoll, was named for Royal Eason Ingersoll, who was a four-star navy admiral. He served as the Atlantic Fleet Commander from 1941 to 1944. The Ingersoll was of the Spruance class which had four General Electric gas- turbine engines that total 80,000 horsepower. She has two screws, which can top the speed of thirty knots with a range of 6,000 nautical miles and a full crew of 296. The Spruance class-destroyer was built to replace the aging WWII destroyers. The primary duty of this class of destroyer was to escort a carrier group. The destroyer has two automatic five-inch guns. She holds two Sikorsky SH 60 Seahawk helicopters. Today, she has a skeleton crew of seven sailors. The two helicopters were being overhauled and not aboard the destroyer.

Chester stood next to the helmsman and watched him turn the destroyer toward the open sea.

Commander Resnis turned to Chester and asked, "Flank speed, Captain?"

"Yes, Commander. Flank speed. How is the Ingersoll fixed for fuel?" Chester raised his left hand up and made a peace sign and then rotated his wrist back and forth with only two fingers raised.

"We are half full." Connie called down to the engine room as she looked at Chester's gesture. "Yes, Captain, the Ingersoll can turn-two. Johnny, give the 'Proud Mary' all she has got. Flank speed."

"Aye, aye, skipper."

Chester asked, "Proud Mary. What do you mean?"

Connie looked straight at Captain Marshall and explained. "The Ingersoll is rather an unconventional destroyer. Have you read Nietzsche's, <u>Thus Spake Zarathustra</u>?"

"No, I haven't, but I have heard of Nietzsche."

Connie answered, "Nietzsche said, life without music would be a mistake. The point is, to boost morale on the ship, instead of getting bored listening to the hum of the ship rattling, we play music. The consensus of the crew was the choice of Creedence Clearwater Revival's song, "*Proud Mary*" the extended version. The crew can focus on their duties more efficiently listening to the music."

"Play it. I like the song. Oh, how many knots can the Ingersoll give us?"

"Close to 40 knots, Captain."

Chester looked at the map. The range from Sasebo to Shanghai looks like just over four hundred nautical miles, which would take the Ingersoll about ten hours to get there.

"Captain," Connie looked directly at Chester and said, "We can get to our destination a little faster than ten hours. She can pull just over forty-five knots."

Chester asked, "How about the weather? Will it be clear sailing?"

Connie replied, "I checked on the weather before you came aboard the Ingersoll. It will be sunny with ten knot winds all the way to Shanghai. The seas will be three-to-five-foot swells."

"Sounds good, Connie." Chester glanced to the open sea and asked, "Oh, you do have a zodiac aboard?"

"Yes, Captain, we do. Would you like some coffee?"

Chester looked at the commander with a grin as he nodded yes. "That would be great and please call me Chester. Use the formality of captain when we are on the shore." Chester was the dean of naval diplomacy. He watched as the commander departed the wheelhouse. Chester glanced ahead and looked at the calm sea. He saw small white caps on three-to-four-foot ocean swells. The morning sun will increase the swells of the ocean. His mind flipped back to his conversation with Admiral Mahone. He was curious why Admiral Mahone did not tell him where his wife, Pilar, was, only that she was on a confidential assignment. He watched as Commander Resnis returned to the wheelhouse with three cups of coffee. One cup for the helmsman. "Thanks, Commander for the coffee." He took a sip from the ship's white coffee cup as he glanced at Commander Resnis. "Tastes good, Connie. Oh, how many sailors do you have on board?"

"We have nine outstanding sailors. The rest of the crew are on shore leave until tomorrow. We have two engineers, John and Steve. Frank is our chef. Of course, we have Henry our helmsman. Bruce is our Radio man. Mike is our weapons man. Howard is our sonarman. Jack is our boatswain mate. Finally, we have Ed, who is our corpsman. Ed will be transferring to Hawaii next week. He is our navy seal." She took a sip of coffee from her mug. "As I understand Chester, you received the Navy Cross." She watched Chester nod his head yes. "If you don't mind me asking you, how did you earn it?"

"I was attached to an Indonesian frigate and to advise the commander of the ship. We were watching a Chinese destroyer dock on the Talaud Island. We told them to leave the island. The Chinese fired the first salvo at us which surprised us by taking out the forward gun and almost blowing out the bridge where I was standing. The skipper of the frigate was knocked unconscious and I was wounded. As we turned around to aim our aft gun at the Chinese destroyer, the Chinese fired another salvo at us and missed. I told the ship we are under fire and to aim the rear gun at the Chinese and keep firing until you knock them out."

"That must have been pretty scary."

"Yes, it was. Oh, how can you get the 'Proud Mary' to turn forty knots?"

"We have a couple of sharp sailors who are very brilliant when it comes to fine tuning engines, diesel or gasoline engines."

"Can you retain these sailors to stay in the navy?"

Connie looked directly at Chester and said, "Unfortunately, these guys are too smart to stay in the navy. They can make more money as civilians."

"I see. Not to change the subject, but why did you choose the navy? "

"I am from Grand Rapids, Ohio which is on the Maumee River. The small city is south of Toledo. We have the Apple Butter Festival, which is kind of neat. Oh, my uncle worked a tugboat on Lake Erie pulling and docking ships in the Cleveland and the Toledo area. I worked on his tugboat for an entire summer and I loved the water and the ships. So, I enrolled at the University of Texas where they had ROTC for the navy. The rest is history. I have been fortunate to have some sharp officers who have guided me in my navy career. I know we have a sharp dedicated crew."

"Good to know."

"By the Chester, is your wife Lieutenant Commander Pilar Marshall?"

Chester smiled at Connie. "Yes. She is my wife."

"I listened to her spot-on assessment of foreign policy of China. She hit the nail on the head. I was impressed by her brilliance on the subject of China. One guy in the audience was a real idiot. He thought he could out smart your wife by talking to her in Mandarin."

"What happened, Connie?"

"Your wife listened to his broken mandarin language and then she corrected his sentences structure in mandarin and she diplomatically told the audience what he said. She then replied to his questions in the Chinese language and repeated her answers to the audience in

English, so we could understand what the guy asked. Chester, I was highly impressed with her knowledge of the Chinese language and of her untangling of the Chinese foreign policy for us. After the lecture, she received a standing applause from everyone in the auditorium."

"I'm glad to hear that from you. Yes, Pilar is very precise."

"Oh, look at the time. For our mid-day lunch, I'm going to make some pier- rogs. I also enjoy cooking."

"What are pier-rogs, Connie?"

"Pier-rogs are a small bun with bits of chopped up ham, bacon bits and bits of onion inside the bun."

"Where did you learn to enjoy cooking?"

"My grandparents came from Riga, Latvia. I believe they arrived in Ellis Island before settling in Ohio. This recipe is from my grandmother. I learned how to make the pier-rogs from her. So, if you would take the conn, so I can make the pier-rogs for all of us."

"I am impressed by your talents, Connie. I have the conn." Chester watched as Connie departed the bridge. He stood holding his coffee cup gazing out from the wheelhouse at the morning sea wondering about his wife, Pilar. He remembered he asked her to lunch and her reply was 'I married you for life, but not for lunch.' He smiled for an instant. He had not seen her in two months. He missed her soft voice and her gentle touch, especially her tender kiss. Chester grinned for a moment as he recalled Pilar's directing him to do a better job at cleaning the dishes. He got used to her annoying him with minor things like that. Chester knew at home he was no longer the captain in the navy, but a lowly Seaman Apprentice. He knew she was perfect in everything she did. Even when she cooked hamburgers they had to be perfectly done. He mentioned to her the world is not perfect and that we all have imperfections. It is the Lords way. He could hear her voice comment 'shine your shoes outside, not in the living room!' As he gazed at the sea in front of him his mind oddly remembered Dusty, his best friend throughout high school. His mind sailed back to a Halloween prank they pulled off one evening. He helped Dusty coil some toilet paper to look like a rope and then stretched it across the country road. They waited for a car to approach the fake rope. This one car stopped in front of the rope and the man got out of his car to look at the rope. As he ripped up the paper rope he heard someone laughing in the bushes. This guy took off running after the prankster. Chester thought it was an opportune moment for a free ride. While the driver was off chasing Dusty, Chester, who was hiding in the bushes on the opposite side of the road walked over to the running car. He opened the car door and sat down in the driver's seat. He felt comfortable sitting in the red leather seat. Chester popped the lever in gear and motored the two-door Cadilac ahead about one hundred feet knowing the driver would return to his car. Chester looked in the rear-view mirror seeing the driver look for his missing parked car. He recalled and smiled as he saw the driver running toward him. Chester remembered he tooted the car's horn and took off leaving the driver high and dry in the dark. Chester drove around and found Dusty. They drove off to Skyway to get some hamburgers and maybe pick up some girls. As the evening was ending, Chester dropped Dusty off and parked the Cadilac a block away leaving the car running with the radio turned up full blast. As he walked home on Castle Boulevard, he knew the neighbors would call the police. Chester recalled he really enjoyed the Halloween evening as he strolled home with a grin on his face.

Chester was going below and meeting Ed, the navy seal. Suddenly, he heard a strong voice behind him.

"Morning Captain. I'm Ed the Hospital Corpsman."

Chester extended his hand to shake with Ed. "Good morning, Ed. I'm pleased to meet you. I'm Captain Chester Marshall." He could feel the vise-like gripe of Ed's powerful handshake.

Ed gave a half smile and asked, "Where might we be going at these knots?"

Chester answered, " I received a call from Admiral Janis Mahone in Hawaii asking if I could help out on picking up a guest off the coast of Shanghai, China."

"Sounds like an important mission. Captain, I would ask that we keep my knowledge of being a seal, quiet. I don't like to boast about being a seal."

"Sure, Ed. Please call me Chester. Leave the Captain on the shore, all right?" Chester paused as he watched Ed nod his head, yes, "I thought you seals worked in teams. Why are you the only one aboard?"

"I was at a conference and then my orders were to the Ingersoll for temporary duty. Next week, I travel back to Hawaii to be with the team."

"I see. Captain Resnis said the Ingersoll has a zodiac aboard. We will probably need the use of it. Could we check it out and make sure the engine works?"

Chester turned to Henry. "Henry, I'm going below. If you need me. Scream. All right?"

Henry nodded and replied, "Aye, aye Captain."

Ed motioned to Chester. "Follow me below." Ed turned exiting the wheelhouse and headed down the ladder to the aft of the destroyer. He heard Chester in tow behind him.

Inside the cabin where the helicopter sits, Chester watched Ed pull the tarp off the zodiac. "How big is it?"

Ed explained, "This zodiac is about fourteen feet long and almost six feet wide. The two outboard engines can reach forty miles per hour. This zodiac has enough gas for sixty miles. She can hold six passengers. Ed aimed his sight from the zodiac to Chester.

Chester turned his eyes from the zodiac to Ed. "Would you be the one driving the zodiac to the pick-up point?"

"Definitely."

Chester watched Ed as he nodded his head with a minor grin.

"It takes only four of us to pick up the zodiac and hoist it over the side."

Chester asked, "Are the engines started by a rope or does the zodiac have electric start for the two engines?"

Ed stood up from a kneeling position and answered, "She has an electric start for both engines."

"When was the last time she was in the water?"

"One week ago. I took the zodiac out for a spin. She performs perfectly."

"Good to know, Ed." Chester looked at his watch. "We have about six more hours until we reach our destination point."

"I'm sure we'll be tracked by our satellites, right? Also, is there a radio frequency which you need to contact once we arrive at our point of destination?"

"Yes, Ed. We'll need to send out our coded message. Have you taken your chief's exam?"

Ed nodded yes. "Just waiting for the results."

"I trust you'll make Chief."

"I hope so," answered Ed. "The operation should run smooth as ice."

Chester crossed his arms on his chest and asked, "Who might be your hero?"

Ed turned away from looking at the zodiac and his sight locked on to Chester's eyes. "It would have to be George Washington."

"Why him?"

"Have you ever heard of the American historian, David McCullough?"

"I don't believe I have."

"He authored a book called, *1776*, in which he drew on George Washington's adventures against the British. The book recounts General Washington's movements in 1776, but only for one year. Washington was a gifted leader. The man had integrity. What is integrity? It is the soundness of ethical character.

Washington did not have a college degree. He only had a fifth or sixth grade education. He was not an intellectual like John Adams. The big note here is that he read a lot of books, which was his learning process. Being six foot two, Washington stood above most of the people in the 1770's. At the age of forty- three weighing about two hundred pounds, he was given command of the continental army. He had no formal training as a general. There was no West Point to train him. He was always clean shaven with an immaculate uniform. "

"I guess I missed this information in my education."

Ed continued, "In January 1776, Henry Knox, who was a bookkeeper in Boston, approached Washington with an idea to drive the British out of Boston. The British were about to burn the city of Boston. The idea was that there would be cannons at Fort Ticonderoga. We could go get them and bring the cannons back to Boston. It was three hundred miles from Boston to Fort Ticonderoga in the dead of winter. There were no highways or restaurants along the way.

Washington authorized Henry Knox and his younger brother to collect the cannons and bring them back to Boston. I am sure Washington thought that Knox would not be able to pull this feat of gathering the cannons and ammunition. This was a monumental feat by Knox who was only 25 years old along with his younger brother who was 19 years old. They had to load up the cannons, the shells and gun powder on numerous wagons and hitch the horses or oxen up to the wagons. They also had to gather feed for the animals, too. Then haul them three hundred miles back to Boston. It wasn't until the middle of March that the cannons arrived and they aligned them up aiming the cannons at the British fleet. The British saw the cannons and asked if they could leave Boston in peace. The British departed on March 17th and sailed their fleet to New York harbor. The British sailed their huge armada which cruised into New York harbor with about 32,000 troops on four hundred man of war and frigate war ships. There was only 2.5 million people living in the colonies predominately in the areas of Boston, New York, Philadelphia and a few cites in the south. By now Washington had moved his troops to New York. Washington's troops were on Staten Island. He had about 9,000 American troops, who were mostly farmers and shop keepers. Washington had just lost over one thousand troops in the battle of Brooklyn. The American troops had no uniforms or hats or even gloves to wear during the winter months. Some had no shoes. George Washington understood his army was out gunned.

The British soldiers were meticulous in their firing their rifles. The British had discipline in their ranks where the young American troops had little training in warfare. Doubt kept creeping into Washington's mind on whether he could beat the British and push them out of the colonies and back to England. Maybe, this war with limited rifles, bullets and ammunition, rationed food, inadequate clothing, not enough money for the troops and untrained men to fight and drive the British out of the colonies was more than he bargained for. Maybe, this effort was too much for one man to control. Possibly, it would be better if he quit and he went back to his estate at Mount Vernon. The Continental Congress said he was the General they needed to force the British from the colonies. The point was that George Washington would not quit. The odds were stacked against him and his limited number of troops. Somewhere, he had the mental strength and strong determination to break through the doubt in his mind and believe against the mounting odds he could beat the British. Washington knew he had to get off the island. It was a matter of hours before the British would attack. If caught, everything would have been lost and he would have been hanged. If he lost, we would have been Canadians or British subjects drinking tea instead of coffee.

Washington would not give up. He had tenacity. His troops looked up to General Washington because he had the mental strength to guide them. How was he going to get off the island away from the British? As luck would have it, it was fate or by the grace of the Lord on the 29th of August 1776, a northern blew in from the north which produced fog on the East River. The British could not sail directly north to the island since the wind was blowing from the north. Now the British could not see beyond the fog and Washington initiated an orderly retreat at night with no lights, no candles. All of the troops had to be quiet as they loaded onto the small boats to cross the East River during the night and into the early morning. As you probably know, there was no American flag at that time. The neat part about it was that Washington was a leader. The men followed him. The men, I'm sure were very hungry. They believed in the cause to get the British out of the colonies. Also. it was the character of Washington that united the colonies to slowly become America. It wasn't the Constitution that united the colonies."

"I never knew this." Remarked Captain Marshall.

Over the load speaker they heard Connie's voice. The pier-rogs are ready. They both headed to the galley.

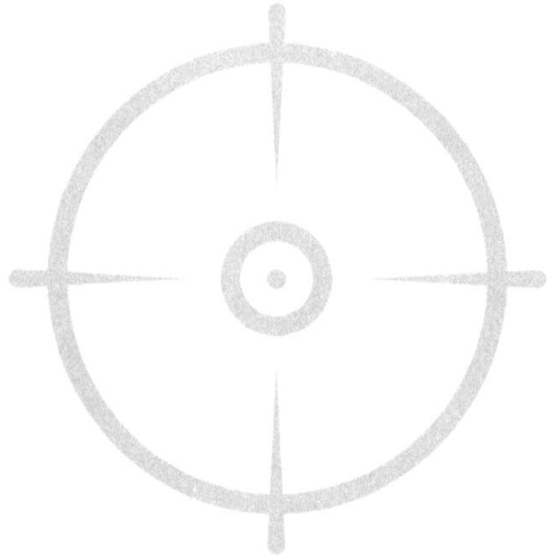

CHAPTER FOURTEEN

Pilar watched Candace hail a taxicab to get them away from the food market.

She was becoming nervous. Being knocked down by an unknown watcher, her shoulder became angry with aggressive throbbing pain. She gently rubbed her shoulder for a moment to relieve the pain. Pilar realized she was walking in unknown spy territory. She was not ready for this adventure in a foreign country. One advantage she had was that she spoke Mandarin. If there was trouble, she could talk her way out of it. She knew Nick was a rookie on this spy journey, too. If needed, Nick would be the muscle she would need against the watcher, if push came to shove. She recognized Nick was eager to help in any way. She would have to rely on Nick's girlfriend, Candace, to get them to the coastline and onto some type of boat which would move them to the rendezvous point somewhere in the ocean. Pilar understood the priority was to get Ming-Li out of the country.

Fortunately, Candace was mature enough to psychologically handle the input of quietly moving Ming-Li out of the country. The element of danger hung with Candace's friend, Margaret. She was the unknown factor. If told about getting Ming-Li out of the country, would Margaret run to the China's secret police and reveal their assignment? If she did run to the authorities, Pilar and Nick would have to move quickly to the Consulate General's office for safety leaving Ming-Li to fend for herself. Then Candace would have to hide from the authorities, too. The mission would have been blown. Pilar needed to ask Candace if Margaret could be trusted by tagging along on this covert assignment. Bluffing Margaret about Candace's boyfriend following them was running thin. Pilar told Candace the better time to let Margaret in on the assignment would be at the marina.

They could leave Margaret at the dock when they sailed away or Margaret could tag along on their fishing adventure. The other x factor was, who was this watcher following them? Pilar did not like constantly looking over her shoulder to see if they would be followed. She felt uncomfortable. Not having a Ph. D from spy school to evade this watcher, Pilar had to gather her flock and run away like a scared rabbit from anyone following them. She looked at her watch and it was getting late in the day. She informed Candace they needed to get to a marina and look for a fishing boat which would get them to the correct longitude and latitude for their rendezvous point offshore. Candace knew of a small boat marina south of Shanghai. Standing on the sidewalk next to the taxi, Pilar informed Candace they would need to get to the marina where they could rent a small boat.

Candace informed the taxi driver they needed to drive to the Fengxian District. Candace told the driver to take toll highway 52 south. Make sure to take the Nanlu Highway south to the Luchaogang Farm. Candace divulged to Pilar it might take one hour to get there because of the traffic jams along the way. Pilar knew at the farm, there should be a waiting fishing boat. Offshore they could pretend they were fishing in the Hangzhou Bay waiting for the sub at a particular longitude and latitude. This journey was becoming increasingly complex. There were too many possibilities that could go wrong, which was not explained to her at the beginning with Admiral Mahone. Pilar would have liked to have waited for the cover of night which would be an aid hiding them from the watcher or even the Chinese security police, but she could not wait until nightfall. She had to get Ming- Li to the rendezvous point by six, today. Pilar hoped the navy submarine would be arriving at the rendezvous point to get them ... away from this ongoing nightmare. This spy escapade was more than Pilar bargained for. This episode was taxing her mind. Across the street, she watched as Candace motioned letting her know a taxi was ready to take them away. Pilar gathered everyone and aimed them at the waiting taxi. Somehow, Pilar remembered she forgot to mail the car payment to the finance company before she left on this assignment. Her mind quickly attached itself to getting into the taxi and getting away. Again, Ming-Li and her mother sat in the front car seat and Candace sat on Nick's lap with Margaret in the middle and Pilar sitting next to the other window seat. Pilar was pleased this next part of the puzzle was completed. Pilar nodded and grinned thanking Candace for her help. As the taxi pulled away from the curb, Pilar looked behind to see if they were being followed. Candace turned and looked through the smoke-stained rear window seeing if they were followed, too. Pilar tried to roll down the passenger window to get some passing air, but the window hand crank broke off. She laid the broken handle on the dirty floor filled with a few torn empty candy wrappers. She glanced at her watch. The time was a little after four.

Outside Pilar noticed the weather was changing from a sunny day to a cloudy day. She wondered if the satellite would be able to pierce through the clouds to locate them in the ocean. As the taxi picked up speed on the highway, Pilar closed her eyes. She wished this adventure would be over. She wondered why the Central Intelligence Agency didn't control this assignment? She thought of her husband, Chester. She missed him. She reached to touch her diamond necklace; the necklace Chester gave her when he proposed. She remembered giving the necklace to Admiral Mahone for safe keeping. She thought when this assignment was over, she would resign her commission in the navy. Her dream of becoming an admiral in the navy was only a fleeting pipe-dream. She hadn't seen her husband in two months. She needed his warm touch. She needed to hear his strong voice. She missed kissing his tender lips and wrapping her arms around him. It wasn't fair being away from him for so long. Pilar loved being Chester's wife. Maybe, she would work on her Master of Business degree at some university. This assignment was more than she bargained for. This assignment of getting Ming-Li out of Shanghai was above her pay grade. She was a duck out of water. If it wasn't for Nick's girlfriend, Candace, helping Pilar snake their way through the city and to the marina, maybe this assignment would have been blown. She knew Candace was intelligent and she loved Nick. Pilar searched her mind wondering who was following them. If it was the Chinese security team, who was watching them, the security team would have captured them by now.

Being caught by the Chinese and sent to prison as a spy is not what Pilar could handle. She thought more time should have been added to this assignment to move Ming-Li safely out of Shanghai. She thought this is not time for self-pity, but to act as a lieutenant commander in the United States Navy and get the job done.

Pilar was resourceful and thankful for Candace's steady support. Suddenly, the taxi slowed down to a crawl and then stopped. They stopped because of an accident on the highway. Another traffic jam. There was no exit off the highway. Pilar looked at her watch. Forty-five minutes had passed by. Mentally, Pilar was growing tired. She was on the edge as she pressed and forced her hands together giving her some form of mental balance and continued strength. The taxi slowly moved forward and gathered speed on the highway. Pilar asked herself, why did she volunteer for this assignment? To advance her naval career or to impress Admiral Mahone? Riding in the taxi, Pilar had time to think which was dangerous. Too much thinking gets one into trouble. Too much analyzation possibly leads to the wrong decision. She trusted Candace. She noticed Margaret was being very quiet in the taxi. Pilar closed her eyes to rest for a moment but her mind kept on thinking. She could not shut her mind off this assignment. Pilar felt a shift in the motion of the taxi. She opened her eyes and saw the highway sign of Nanlu. The taxi driver turned south. They were getting closer to the marina. She noticed Ming-Li was very quiet sitting in the front passenger's seat with her mother. Pilar thought maybe Ming-Li would change her mind defecting to America once they were at the fishing dock.

Margaret turned to Candace and asked, "Why are we going to the marina? This does not make any sense to me."

Candace replied, "We are going fishing."

"Why?" demanded Margaret.

Candace leaned forward and looked at Pilar. "Should we tell her?"

Pilar answered, "Does the driver speak English?" She did not want the driver to know of their movement.

Candace replied, "No, only Mandarin."

"All right. Go ahead and tell her."

Candace explained in English. "Margaret, we are traveling to the marina to get Ming-Li on a fishing boat. Someone will pick her up and take her away."

"So where are they taking her?"

"She is wanting to go to America."

"What?"

"You heard me, Margaret." Candace paused looking at her, "America."

"So how is she getting to America? Why don't you take her to the airport?"

Candace calmly placed her arm around her girlfriend's shoulder and whispered softly into Margaret's ear. "She is defecting to America. She hates China. Do you understand what I am saying and keep this quiet to yourself." She saw Margaret's eyes grow larger and nod her head yes.

In Mandarin, Margaret whispered to Candace, *"So, Pilar is helping get Ming-Li and her mother out of China?"*

Pilar leaned over to Candace, "Let me answer her, all right?" She watched Candace nod her head, yes. In perfect Mandarin language Pilar replied to Margaret's question. *"Nick and I are here to escort Ming-Li to a rendezvous point in the ocean. She has had enough of China's human abuse. She can't fly away. The only way is to get her to a rendezvous point off the coast. Understand?"* She watched as Margaret's eyes grew wider as her mouth opened without a smile with this surprisingly added information.

In English Margaret replied. "I did not know you spoke Mandarin. So, you heard everything I said about you and Nick?"

"That is correct, Margaret. I would ask that you remain calm and help us with escorting Ming-Li and her mother to our rendezvous point in the ocean, all right? Or you can stay at the marina."

"Yes, yes, I will. But how is she getting away in the ocean?"

"By a submarine."

"Oh my."

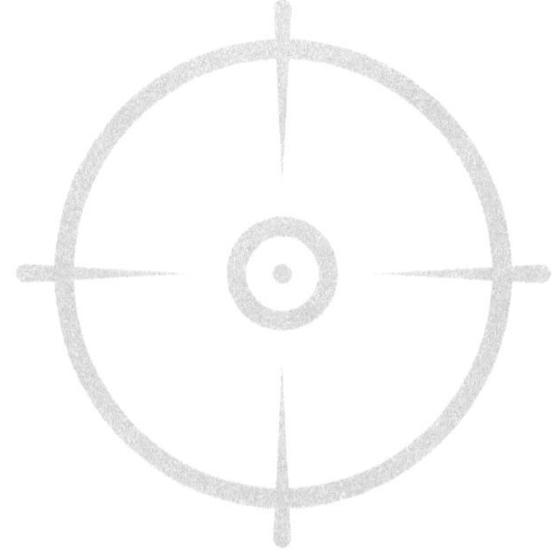

CHAPTER FIFTEEN

usty listened to the dial tone waiting for Admiral Mahone to pick up the receiver. He was becoming nervous from the CNN news report regarding the missing Chinese official. Maybe, the Chinese were looking for someone other than Ming-Li.

Admiral Mahone was relieved she reached Captain Marshall informing him to pick up a guest off the coast of Shanghai, China. She was still fuming about the rudeness of Admiral Ambrose. She thought the man was incompetent. He did not deserve stars on his shoulder boards. She was ready to leave her office for the evening when the telephone rang. "Admiral Mahone. May I help you?"

"Hi Admiral Mahone, this is Dusty Sommers."

"Evening, Dusty."

"Did you hear the Chinese are looking for their missing high-ranking government official?"

"No. I have not. But there is a little twist with the picking up of our guest."

"What's the problem?" Dusty asked.

"Admiral Ambrose who is the head of all the submarines in the Pacific Fleet learned about the use of the USS Connecticut to pick up our guest off the coast of Shanghai, China."

"So."

"He halted the movement of the Connecticut which was on her way to the rendezvous point. Unfortunately, he would not listen to reason."

"Oh, no!" Dusty closed his eyes and exhaled. "I don't believe this has happened." Dusty immediately launched his anger over the phone, "Admiral, there is no contingency plan or an alternate plan for the team to deviate from. This was just a simple extraction to get Ming-Li out of Shanghai. We cannot have the extraction team waiting and wondering on where is the submarine!"

Admiral Mahone listened to Dusty's reality of the extraction team. "We are not sunk, yet Dusty. I reached Captain Marshall in Sasebo, Japan. Sasebo is less than five hundred miles from Shanghai. He was able to collect a ship and travel at flank speed to the rendezvous point."

"How is he going to pick up our guest inside Chinese waters? Only a submarine could sneak into their waters." Dusty paused. "Besides, it will take him too much time to get there as compared to a sub. He'll be late picking them up at the rendezvous point. They will not be able to wait on the water for the ship to pick them up. The Chinese coastal-shore security will spot them. The game will be over. Pilar and Nick will be arrested." Dusty hesitated. "Who is this other admiral who chopped you in half?"

Janis answered, "Admiral Ambrose. He is a four-star admiral."

"Not to worry, Dusty. Captain Marshall's ship will remain in international waters while their small zodiac boat will travel to the coordinates to pick up our guest."

"Who is Ambrose's boss?"

"The Chief of Naval Operations, Admiral Taylor."

"I was hoping some foul up like this would not happen." There was irritation in his voice. Dusty looked down at his desk. His eyes were searching for relief. "I hope you are right, Admiral Mahone. Have you ever heard of Murphy's law?"

"No, I have not."

"What can go wrong, will go wrong." Dusty continued, "I'll have to contact my boss about this interruption. Thank you for your information Admiral." Dusty hung up the phone. He immediately dialed his director at his home in Virginia.

"Evening Director, this is Dusty."

The Director listened to the annoyance in Dusty's voice. "Hi Dusty. What's wrong?" asked Director Laube as he puffed on his cigar.

"CNN reported that the Chinese are missing and looking for one of their high- ranking government officials. They might be looking for our guest."

"Yes, I heard the news report."

"A few moments ago, I talked to Admiral Mahone. She commented that the submarine in which they were to use to extract our guest was rerouted to another assignment. They will not send another submarine."

"Why was the transport terminated?"

"Evidently, Mahone's senior admiral terminated the use of the transport."

"Who is this other admiral?"

"She said it was Admiral Ambrose."

"Is the navy sending another transport?"

"Yes, sir. She got hold of Captain Marshall in Sasebo, Japan. It wasn't a submarine."

"Sounds like they might be late to the rendezvous point?" asked the Director.

"I hope not." Remarked Dusty.

"Do we know who is Admiral Ambrose's boss?"

"I would say the Chief of Naval Operations, Admiral Taylor."

"All right. I'll give him a shout. Thank you, Dusty. Good evening."

Dusty heard the phone go dead. He saw Dianne's head pop into his office. "I'll be right there for dinner."

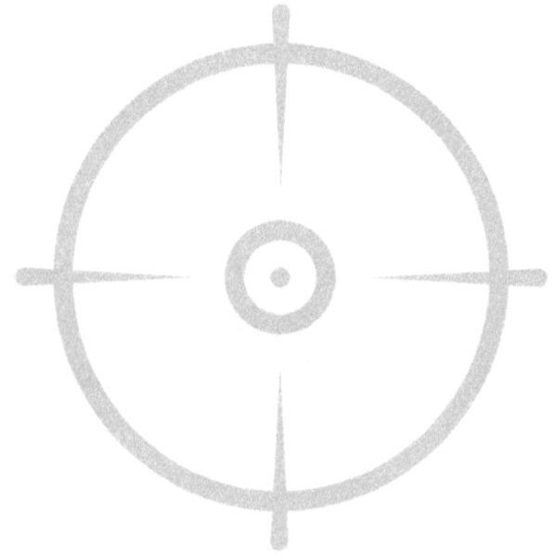

CHAPTER SIXTEEN

Director Von Laube leafed through his naval directory and found the CNO's telephone number. He punched the digits on the phone and listened for the ring. "Good evening Admiral Taylor. This is Director Von Laube from the Alexander Hamilton Foundation."

"Good evening, Director. How may I help you?"

"I received a call from our Operation's manager. There was a plan to extract a guest from Shanghai, China. He talked to Admiral Mahone. She orchestrated a submarine to be sent to retrieve the guest. Evidently, Admiral Ambrose intervened in the authorization of the submarine. Now, we have our team who will be waiting for a submarine to pick them up. Unfortunately, there will be no submarine to extract them. Admiral Mahone selected an alternative to extract the team. I thought the navy is supposed to assist our clandestine operations?" The Director paused to collect his angered thoughts. He continued, "Didn't the Secretary of the Navy, Golwaz, say the navy would assist in any covert operation? I believe you were in that meeting six months ago, right? Or am I mistaken?"

"Yes, sir. I was there in the meeting."

"Good to hear your confirmation, Admiral Taylor." In a deeper tone Director Laube asked, "Then why was Admiral Mahone's request of a submarine denied? Was it because of an inept Admiral Ambrose, who did not want to listen to one of your qualified lady admirals? Or did you instruct Admiral Ambrose to stab our extraction operation in the back? You know, we have people relying on a submarine to pick them up today and now there will be no submarine. I want an answer from you, Admiral Taylor, before, I call our President about the navy's screw-up."

"Director Laube, there will be no need for you to call the President. I will call Admiral Ambrose and get a submarine to your extraction point. Also, I will call Admiral Janis Mahone and inform her of the correction. Your team will have their submarine."

"You'll do this correction, now, Admiral Taylor?"

"Yes, sir."

"Thank you for your assistance. Goodbye." Director Laube hung up the phone.

He called Dusty and explained to him Admiral Taylor is sending a submarine.

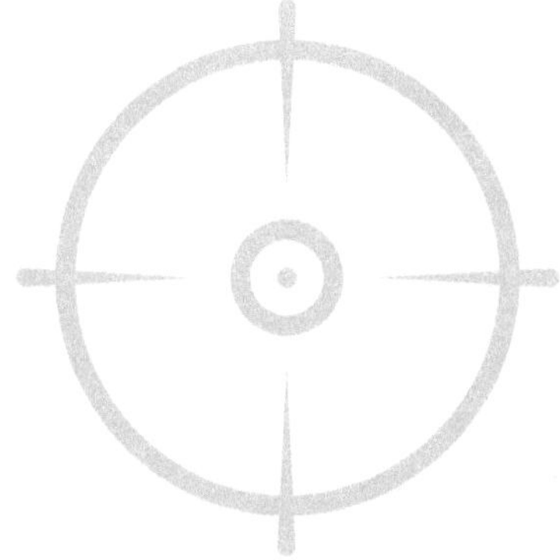

CHAPTER SEVENTEEN

Admiral Taylor grit his teeth. He was a fair admiral with excellent judgement. What he did not tolerate was insubordination. He was always direct and to the point. He did not play games with other peoples' emotions. The admiral did not use bad language only his deep growl moving his sailors to the correct speed, proper course and a straight direction. Admiral Taylor was a big heavy man standing over six foot tall. Many sailors were afraid of his commanding presence.

He located and grabbed his naval directory. He found Admiral Ambrose's telephone number and dialed it.

"Good evening Admiral Ambrose, this is Taylor."

"Good evening Admiral."

"Let me get to the point. Did you correct the direction of one of our submarines after talking to Admiral Janis Mahone?"

"I certainly did. She had no authorization to use one of my submarines."

"Did you know the use of the sub was for a covert operation?"

"Yeah, I did. Why?"

"Why did you terminate her request?"

"She had no authorization. She did not ask me for the use of one of my submarines."

"And, because she did not ask you for the use of the submarine, you decided to chop here request. Did you know that the submarine was going to be used for a secret extraction?"

"I sure did. Our sub was to travel to the coast of Shanghai, China. I was not going to allow one of my subs to be possibly caught inside the coastal waters of China."

"I understand your point, Admiral; however, did you know this was a secret assignment?"

"Yeah. I did." Replied an incensed Ambrose. He listened to the CNO's growl over the telephone. "What? You're hot at me for not complying with Admiral Mahone's request?"

"I sure am Admiral. There are people at the extraction point waiting to be picked up by our sub. So, what are they to do? Paddle around in the water, waiting for one of our submarines which will not arrive?

"That is not my problem?"

"Whose problem is it, Admiral?"

Admiral Ambrose responded, "They should have thought about an alternative extraction."

"No, Admiral Ambrose, wrong answer! Here is what I am ordering you to do. You will get in touch with that sub in Hawaii which you turned around and get that submarine to the coordinates which Admiral Janis Mahone instructed the sub to pick up the extraction team off the coast of Shanghai, China." In a demanding and loud voice, Admiral Taylor barked, "I want this done right now. Got It!"

"Are you sure you want to do this? What if the sub gets caught?"

"As sure as the silver stars are on my collar, Admiral Ambrose."

"What if I refuse?"

"Admiral Ambrose, our sub commanders are that good they will not get caught. Do you understand my drift, sailor?"

"No, I will not send our sub off the coast of China."

"Who is your second in command?"

"Admiral Ben Franklin."

"Admiral Ambrose, you are relieved of your command and you have been reduced in rank for refusing my order. You just lost one star from your collar. I will contact the Bureau of Personnel and instruct them to reduce you from a four-star admiral down to a three-star admiral. Also, you'll need to get your ID changed, too. Got it?"

"Yeah. I'm calling the Inspector General about this." Suddenly, Admiral Ambrose hung up the telephone connection.

Admiral Taylor grit his teeth and mumbled to himself, 'what an idiot.' He hung up the telephone and looked up Ben Franklin's phone number. He immediately dialed his number. "Good evening Admiral Franklin."

"Good evening Admiral Taylor."

"Admiral Ambrose is relieved of his command and reduced in flag rank from four- stars down to three- stars."

"I understand."

"There was a sub which Admiral Ambrose turned around today, right?"

"Yes, sir. The submarine was the USS Connecticut."

"I am ordering you to send another sub on its original task to pick up our secret team off the coast of Shanghai, China. I want this done, immediately. Can you do this?"

"Yes, sir. I can send the North Carolina on this mission."

"Who is the sub commander?'

"Commander Dave Griggs. He is an outstanding sub driver."

"Good to hear. Make sure you inform Commander Griggs to drive the North Carolina with flank speed to the pickup point. Admiral Franklin, you are temporarily in command of the Pacific submarine fleet."

"Aye, aye, sir."

Admiral Taylor hung up the phone. He punched in the phone number to Admiral Janis Mahone. "Good evening Janis. This is Taylor."

"Good evening, Admiral."

"I just got off the phone with Admiral Franklin. I directed him to send the North Carolina to the original rendezvous point for this covert mission."

"May I ask what changed?"

"I had a serious discourse with Admiral Ambrose and ordered him to send the Connecticut to the rendezvous point. He flatly refused. I immediately removed him from his command of the Pacific sub fleet and he is now reduced to a three- star admiral."

"I see." Janis paused with a tinge of a grin on her face. "Thank you Admiral for your help in sending the North Carolina to the pickup point. I have contacted Captain Marshall in Sasebo and he is on the way to Shanghai, but he will remain in international waters. He'll use a zodiac to collect the team."

"If the zodiac can't collect the team, you'll have the original backup of the North Carolina to collect the team. The sub might be a little late, but the sub will arrive at the rendezvous point."

"Thank you Admiral Taylor."

"If you have any further questions, please let us know. Good night."

Janis heard the phone go dead. She placed the receiver down. She was relieved the CNO intervened. "Just deserts." Janis paused for a moment. "This calls for a bottle of white wine for dinner, tonight." She logged off her computer and turned the lights off in her office and headed home.

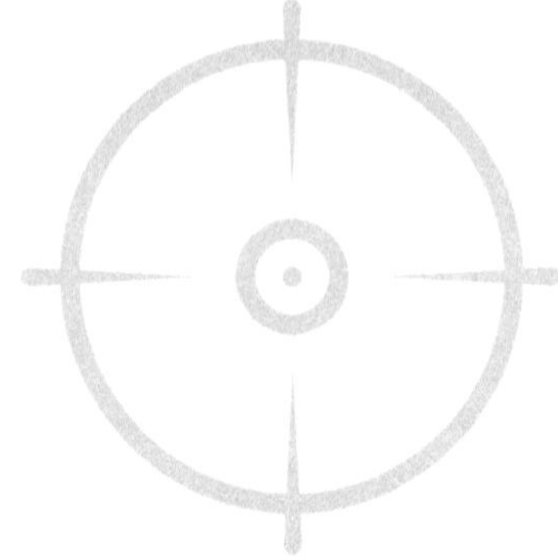

CHAPTER EIGHTEEN

Sitting next to Margaret, who was very quiet during the taxi ride to the coast, Pilar felt cramped sitting in the back seat of the taxi. Looking ahead, Pilar viewed the blue ocean and the approaching overhead clouds. A small smile fell upon her face. One more hurdle to go. She had to find a fishing boat to carry them to the coordinates off the coast of Shanghai. She could smell the fresh salt air from the ocean. She was relieved they made it this far. The taxi stopped at the end of the dirt road. Pilar exited the taxi and looked behind her. Hopefully, the watcher disappeared. She only saw a guy on a noisy motorcycle headed toward them. Pilar watched as Candace opened the other passenger door of the taxi, she too looked behind the taxi to see if they were being followed. Candace looked over to Pilar with a plain face. They both saw no signs of the watcher. Pilar turned toward the ocean. She inhaled the fresh ocean air. She missed Chester's smooth tanned face, his warm smile and his tender touch. She had enough of this spy business. She wanted this adventure to be over. Pilar watched as Nick step out of the taxi. He looked around and saw no watcher. Ming-Li and her mother departed the taxi.

Margaret was out of the taxi and pointed toward the ocean. Pilar paid the taxi driver. After they watched the taxi depart, they all strolled toward the boat dock, which was fifty yards away. There were a few boats tied to the wooden pier. Pilar did not see anyone around. She glanced to her right and saw numerous plants growing in straight rows. She could see a farmhouse off in the distance. She turned to her left side and observed a small wooden cottage painted white. She thought maybe the boat owners were sitting in the cottage.

Pilar concentrated on her final chore. She walked over to the empty boats. Nick and Candace followed. There was what appeared to be four twenty foot open- sized boats moored to the pier. They stepped onto the four-foot-wide wooden pier which stretched out about sixty feet and looked inside the first two boats.

One boat had six to twelve inches of standing water in the hull. The second boat had no motor. Pilar could not believe this. She advanced her view on the third boat. It had an outboard motor. She did not see a gas tank inside the boat. She could not believe her luck. She walked forward to view the fourth boat. The fourth boat had a small cabin and an outboard engine with a gas tank sitting in the hull. She wondered if it had any gasoline in the tank. Pilar noticed the new Honda outboard engine sitting on the back of the fourth boat. Pilar looked around toward the cottage to see if anyone was around. Nick, Candace and Margaret walked back toward the cottage with hopes someone could start the engine and get them to the rendezvous point.

Candace and Nick talked to the boat owner and informed him they would like to go fishing for a small time. Candace looked at Nick and said, "This is Johnny. He is the boat captain. He wants two thousand dollars to take us fishing, today. Is that a suitable number for you?" Candace watched Margaret pick up the telephone and call someone. She thought that was interesting. Who would she be calling?

"Sure." Nick exited the cottage to let Pilar know they would need two thousand dollars to rent the boat. Pilar handed Nick the dollar amount. Nick walked back to the cottage and gave the money to Candace.

Candace told Johnny the dollar amount would be fine and handed him the two thousand dollars. Johnny informed her he would have to get some gasoline for the boat. Candace walked toward Pilar and told Pilar the boat captain had to get some gasoline. She also let Pilar know Margaret telephoned someone. She watched Pilar nod her head.

"Great. More time delay." Pilar asked Candace, "Did he have any fishing bait?"

"Yes. He had the fishing bait," Candace answered.

They watched Johnny pick up the gasoline can and head off on foot to get the can filled with fuel. Pilar could see the gas station was about one hundred yards away. Pilar looked at her watch. It read five thirty. She looked at Nick and said, "We are cutting this close. Our rendezvous time is at six o'clock."

Nick looked out toward the ocean. He felt a cool breeze coming offshore. The clouds continued to roll in. He saw what appeared to be fog a mile offshore.

"Pilar, do you see what I see offshore?"

Pilar turned to realize what Nick was seeing. Fog. "How are they going to see us in that fog?"

Candace turned to hug Nick. She whispered in his ear. "I'm getting scared."

Nick said, "There is nothing to be scared about. All we are going to do is motor out to the coordinates and a sub will surface. We'll drop off Ming-Li and her mother. The submarine will slip away unnoticed. Pilar will go with them. The assignment will be over. You can stay here on the dock if you wish with Margaret."

"No. I'll go with you and Pilar."

Pilar was always a perfect person. From her earning straight A's in high school through her graduating from the University of Texas to her easily learning the Chinese language in the navy, things went smoothly for her. But now, all of her superlative grades from her education would not give her the advantage she required in this situation. She needed a good dose of pragmatics which would aid her in this new setting. This assignment was not going smoothly. She did not enjoy this covert assignment. Somehow, her mind quickly flipped back to sipping a fine California Merlot wine with her husband, Chester. There was no time to think of her husband. Pilar had to untangle and grab hold of this reality. The Alexander Hamilton Foundation was counting on her, especially Dusty. She did not want to fail in this assignment and lose face with Admiral Mahone. She knew Ming-Li trusted her to get her out of China, safely. She looked to see if the captain of the boat was walking back with a can of gasoline. She did not see him. She asked herself what is taking him so long? She glanced at her watch. It read five forty-five. Time was running out. She did not want to be late to the rendezvous point. She did not want to think of the possibility if they missed the opportunity for Ming-Li to escape. She gazed at Margaret. She saw that she was calm. Pilar watched Margaret walk over to and look at the rows of green strawberry plants. Pilar noticed Candace was a little nervous. She stood close to Nick not wanting to leave his side. Ming-Li and her mother were standing and peering out at the ocean. Ming-Li never said too much during this adventure. Pilar scanned the ocean horizon and did not see another boat. She asked Nick to look at the fourth boat to see if the boat had any life jackets. Nick returned informing Pilar there were three life jackets aboard the boat. He looked at the other three boats and there were no extra life jackets.

Pilar asked, "Nick, do you think the fourth boat will get us to the rendezvous point without fail?"

"I'm sure it will, Pilar. I did not see any water laying in the hull." Nick looked out at the ocean surveying the weather conditions. "The only thing that bothers me is the oncoming fog." He hesitated. "Pilar, how far do we have to travel to meet the submarine?"

She held up her wristwatch. "The watch will beep once we reach the rendezvous point. Then we wait. You know the navy, hurry up and wait."

"At least you get to leave with Ming-Li and her mother while I stay behind. Hopefully, you will not be seen by anyone on the shore."

"I'm sure we will not be spotted by anyone on the shore. You know Pilar, studying you these past hours, you remind me of two outstanding actors who really stand out in my mind. Barbara Stanwyck and Betty Davis."

"Thanks Nick, but why those two actresses?"

"The other day, as I watched a *Perry Mason* rerun, where he was not in that one particular show, Betty Davis was in the TV show. She was the lawyer with the help of Paul Drake in this one episode. She was a formidable lawyer. She did not faulter even though she had to fight an uphill battle looking for evidence to clear her client. She had strength as you do, Pilar. And with Barbara Stanwyck, who played on *The Big Valley*, she had a commanding performance running the ranch. She knew what to do, as you do, Pilar." Nick grinned.

"Thanks, Nick. Nice of you to compare me to two award winning actresses." Pilar looked to see if the captain was walking back with a can of gasoline. She did not see him. She looked at Candace and Nick. "Thanks to you both for your immediate help on this assignment."

Candace asked, "Nick said you are a lieutenant commander in the navy. Is that right?"

"Yes, Candace. I volunteered for this covert mission. It seemed like an easy assignment. I did not expect these various hurdles along the way. I did not mean to drag you and Margaret into this journey."

"Oh, it's no trouble. I'm pleased to help you. I hope we don't get caught by the Chinese shore security. They usually come by every hour."

"Nick, what time do you have?"

"It is six o'clock, Pilar."

"We should be at the rendezvous point, by now. I'm sure the sub has its periscope up looking for us. I'm sure they won't wait too long for us."

Nick viewed the guy walking with the gasoline can. He pointed to him. "There, the guy is walking back with the gas."

Pilar turned to the guy carrying the gasoline can. "Finally!"

They watched as Johnny waltzed on the wooden pier to the fourth boat and climbed into the boat. He poured the gas into the boat's fuel tank. He then walked back carrying the empty gas can to the cottage. He reappeared with a small container of fishing bait and several fishing poles. He motioned for all of them to go to the boat.

Nick reassured and mentioned to Pilar that the boat should make it out to the rendezvous point. "It's only a mile or so, right?" Nick noticed the varnish was peeling off the mahogany wood and the hull needed a nice white paint job. Nick knew the twenty-foot boat needed maintenance. He could not wait to get back to the apartment and start reading his navigation book.

"I hope Nick." Pilar walked everyone to the wooden dock. She was pleased the boat was ready to be launched. She watched as Ming-Li and her mother stepped aboard and sat in the middle of the boat. Margaret stepped into the boat and sat behind Ming-Li. Candace was next to enter the boat and sat down next to Margaret on the unvarnished wooden seat. She looked up at Nick. She saw him staring back at the shoreline.

"Oh, no." Nick said as he gazed at this guy who was walking toward them fifty yards away.

Pilar watched Nick's face turn from a pleasing grin to an unpleasing glare.

"What is it Nick?"

"Look behind us." He kept his steady and constant glare at the oncoming unknown person.

Pilar turned and looked at the person with the blue baseball cap wearing large sunglasses approaching them. Her heart increased its rhythm. "How did he find us?" She knew this time there was no way they could outrun the watcher.

Maybe, they could cast off and still get away. She told the captain of the boat to start the engine. "Nick, get in the boat, now!" The watcher was now twenty-five yards from the dock. She could see the watcher pick up his pace as he walked toward them. She saw something dark in his hand. Sitting in front of the captain, she turned behind her watching the captain as he pulled on the rope to start the engine. The outboard engine would not start. After the fifth pull on the cord, Pilar barked, "Pull the choke!" She saw the captain look at her with a smile and pulled the choke. He yanked on the cord. The engine snapped awake. Another hurdle was accomplished. She untied the aft boat line and pushed the boat away from the dock. The outboard engine was humming. She watched as Nick stretched forward to untie the bow line. Pilar heard the watcher say, "Stop right there!" Her eyes froze on the watcher. She saw him pointing his gun at them.

"Everybody, out of the boat!" The watcher stood like a statute on the dock as he ordered them out motioning with his gun.

The rear of the boat had swung away from the dock. The bow line was still tied to the cleat on the dock. Pilar thought someone had leaked their mission. How else was the watcher to follow them. She could not believe the game was over.

Pilar was counting on Nick to do something. She saw Nick grab hold of the wooden oar laying in the boat and hand one end of the oar to the watcher, so the boat could swing back to the dock. As the boat slowly moved back to the dock, Pilar saw the watcher pull on the boat oar while Nick held on to the other end of the oar. Nick placed one foot onto the dock to jump up on the dock while his other leg steadied himself on the boat. The watcher held the boat oar firmly in his hand as Nick moved onto the dock. As fast as a lightning bolt would flash, Nick quickly moved the end of the boat oar which the watcher was holding and shoved the watcher's end of the oar into his stomach. He heard the watcher moan. The boat swung back and bumped into the dock.

Johnny reached out to hold onto the wooden dock. Nick pushed the oar as hard as he could into the watcher's stomach. The watcher bent forward. The sudden thrust of the oar into the stomach of the watcher was unexpected. Nick did not stop his swift and his powerful attack as he climbed on the wooden pier moving the watcher backwards. Nick saw the watcher was off balance and falling backwards. The watcher raised his head to glance at Nick. Nick with determination continued his forward momentum of force toward the watcher. The watcher's heel of his foot caught the cleat on the dock which made him fall off the pier and backwards into the other boat which was tied to the dock. As a reflex, the watcher pulled the trigger of his gun. The gun discharged a loud pop. Everyone watched him fall backwards into the empty boat. The watcher's head slammed hard onto the wooden rail of the boat. The watcher moaned as his hand released the oar from his grip. Pilar could see Nick grab his side and he immediately dropped to the wooden dock. The oar flew out of his hands. The oar fell banging onto the wooden deck. She saw he was in burning pain. Pilar climbed up on the dock and into the other boat where the watcher was moaning. She pulled his gun from his hand and took off his glasses to get a good look at the watcher. She did not know him. She climbed back onto the dock looking at Nick. Nick was laying on his back and he was moaning holding his chest. She saw the advancing wet blood growing on one side of his shirt. She heard Candace shout his name.

"Nick!" Again, Candace heard his loud moan.

"Oh. It hurts. My side." Nick remained on his back. He held his upper chest. He felt something wet.

No one in the boat could believe Nick was shot. No one screamed. They sat in disbelief.

Pilar watched Candace climb out of the boat and move toward Nick stretched out on the dock. They could not believe this happened. Candace looked at Pilar.

Pilar quickly looked into the boat for any cloth or rag to stop the bleeding. She saw one dirty rag laying on the floor of the boat. She shook her head, no. She looked back at Candace. "Candace, take off your bra and place it underneath Nick's shirt. It will slow down the bleeding." She watched as Candace slip off her bra underneath her white polo shirt. She wasn't bashful as she handed it to Pilar. Pilar pulled up Nick's cloth shirt to look at the wound on his chest. She hoped the bullet did not enter his chest. If the bullet entered his chest cavity, then it would be game over. Candace and Pilar viewed the wound as it oozed brightly colored red blood from the right side of his upper chest. They could see a small portion of Nick's white rib bone. Apparently, the bullet grazed the right side of his upper rib cage tearing open the skin and ripping-apart about one inch of the muscle tissue. Pilar took hold of Candace's bra and folded it placing the bra on the wound. "Nick, hold this on your chest. This will stop the bleeding." They watched as Nick held the bra over his wound. She told Candace to apply pressure to the wound.

"What do we do now?" Candace asked.

Nick said, "We go on. Get me up and into the boat. Let's go."

Pilar asked, "Are you sure, Nick?"

"Yeah. This really hurts. At least the bullet did not kill me. We need to get her to the rendezvous point." Nick inched his way off the dock onto the boat.

They watched as Johnny climbed out of the boat. "I want no part of this!"

They watched Johnny walk back to shore. Hopefully, he would not call the security police.

Margaret quietly sat wide-eyed in the boat and could not believe this incident happened.

Pilar said, "We'll bring the boat back to you." The fifty horsepower Honda motor was humming. She helped Nick into the boat. He sat next to Candace holding his pulsing wound. Pilar stepped to the back of the boat next to the motor. "Ming-Li, untie the bow line." She watched her untie the line and sit back down. Pilar pulled the lever to set the motor in forward gear. Her hand turned the throttle of the motor to full power. She thought to herself, 'What could happen next'? She pushed the boat away from the dock. Pilar commented, "After we pass the stone breakers in about thirty seconds, we'll be in the ocean headed to our rendezvous point." Pilar sat holding on the throttle hoping Nick would survive this assignment. When he goes to the hospital later, he'll have to answer a lot of questions from the Chinese police on how and where he was shot. Candace would have to back up his story. As the boat cleared the stone breakers, the boat was now cutting through the three-to-five-foot swells. "All right everybody, hold on to your seats. It is going to get a little bumpy." The wooden boat was bouncing from a three-foot wave to the next larger wave. The front of the boat sprayed a constant mist of water onto the faces of everyone. Pilar knew Nick could not take the pounding of the waves at this fast pace of the boat. Pilar decreased the throttle which made the boat gently cut through the waves at an easier pace. She was waiting for the beep on her watch to tell her they were at the correct rendezvous point. She prayed the submarine was watching them from their periscope. Off in the distance, she could see the fog bank straight ahead. The fog bank was about a half mile away. She looked to her left and saw a dark dot on the horizon. The dot was about three hundred yards away. She wondered if it was the mast of a Chinese patrol boat or a fishing boat? She had enough of this friction.

Pilar wanted this nightmare to end. She heard Nick say it was hard to breathe. "Ming-Li, you and your mother put on the life jackets." She asked Margaret, "Can you swim?"

"I can dog paddle."

"Good enough. Candace can you swim?"

"No. I can't swim."

"Okay. Put on the other life jacket." Pilar watched Candace grab the other jacket and put it on. She turned her wrist to see what time it was. Her watch read six twenty. Pilar searched the surrounding ocean for a submarine. She kept motoring forward hoping the watch would beep letting her know they were at the correct rendezvous location. She thought, maybe the watch is not operating properly and they are at the wrong location offshore. She glanced to her left and saw the previous black dot had now turned and headed toward them. It appeared to Pilar the oncoming boat was a patrol boat not a fishing boat. She thought for sure the patrol boat had their binoculars eyeing them. "Ming- Li. Get hold of the fishing bait and hook a fish on the hook. Then get the line over the side. Pretend we are fishing, All right?" Pilar watched as Ming-Li placed the fishing bait on the hook and threw it over the side of the boat.

"Pilar, can you head toward the fog bank? We can disappear in the fog," Nick asked.

Pilar continued their forward movement straight toward the fog bank. She was not scared, but nervous. She added more power to their Honda outboard motor to reach the fog bank to hide from the patrol boat advancing on them. She placed the gun on the deck next to her foot.

The tone of Pilar's voice was commanding. Usually, she had a soft tone when she spoke, but now as her eyes searched in the solid white, grey fog for the submarine, she could not hear over the constant engine noise. She thought maybe the submarine surfaced. She turned off the engine noise and listened. She heard the ocean lap against the hull of the boat. "Quiet everyone." She could hear off in the distance the Chinese patrol boat's motor humming along searching for them in the dense fog. Without warning, her watch beeped, Pilar said to herself, 'We made it.' They reached the rendezvous point for pick up. She gently touched Candace on her arm who sat in front of her and softly said, "Candace, we are at the location for our rendezvous. Can you tell Ming-Li?" She watched as Candace leaned forward and quietly told Ming-Li they had reached their pickup point.

Candace turned to ask Pilar, "What do we do now?" Candace continued to hold Nick in her lap holding pressure on this wound.

"We wait." Pilar realized in a few hours it would be dark. There was no way the sub could find them in this fog at night. She bet the Chinese patrol boat had a powerful search light which could find them in the fog at night. If the sub did not locate them in the next few hours, she would have to motor back to shore and hide. She watched as Nick forced himself to sit up holding his side. She noticed Margaret was searching for the sub in the fog and listening, too.

At the rendezvous point searching for the submarine, Pilar was not apprehensive or worried hunting through the fog. She remembered Admiral Mahone said the submarine will pick you up. She relied on what the admiral said. She trusted the admiral, but the fear of being caught by the Chinese patrol boat began to weigh on her mind. She glanced down at the pistol next to her foot. She knew the pistol would be no match against a machine gun from the Chinese patrol boat. She happened to remember, when she gazed into Chester's eyes, his bold eyes gave her strength. His eyes gave her courage. His powerful eyes handed her a platform to stand on and deliver. Pilar concentrated on remembering his blue eyes focusing on her, which gave her the electricity and passion to move ahead. However, the fear of not being picked up by the sub began to creep into her mind. She realized it has been a good twenty minutes searching for the submarine. She thought what if the submarine left the rendezvous location because of the Chinese patrol boat? Pilar knew from her naval training if fear took over in any situation then panic comes next blocking your common sense. This formidable fear was knocking at the outskirts of her naval reasoning. This fear was demanding to simply stroll into her mind. This fear was waiting for the invitation to proudly march into Pilar's head. This fear was free for the taking. This fear was hungry for Pilar. Fear's cousin panic was waiting in the background. Panic kept on pushing this fear to move forward. Panic was pleased to follow fear. Panic was millimeters away from fear. Pilar wanted out of this reality. She had to control this nightmare by having the faith the navy would not let her down. She kept her eyes searching for the submarine. The fog was thick. Pilar would hold her sight for a moment to the left side of the boat searching for the sub and then focus her sight to the right side hoping to see the submarine. The black color of the submarine would stand out in the fog. She heard the sound of the patrol boat slowly motoring, advancing closer ahead of them. The patrol boat sounded like it was headed straight for them. She saw Candace turn her head toward Pilar. Pilar could see the fear growing on Candace's face. Margaret turned her head looking at Pilar for guidance. Pilar offered a small grin on her face as she gently rubbed and tapped Candace's shoulder. Giving Candace some evidence of the strength of safety. Pilar tapped the shoulder of Margaret, too. The touch from Pilar's hand gave comfort to a nervous Candace and Margaret. Moments later, they heard the patrol boat gradually turn and change its course passing one hundred feet away from them. The patrol boat disappeared in the fog. Their fear faded. Their search for the sub continued.

Water droplets from the fog dampened everyones' clothes. Everyone's hair was full of moisture from the fog. Pilar knew this thick fog was saving them from certain capture. The temperature in August was 88 degrees. The water temperature on the coast was roughly 80 degrees. Pilar thought if the patrol boat comes closer, she knew they could start the Honda motor and send their boat in the opposite direction where the patrol boat would follow it in the fog wanting to capture them, while they all slipped from their boat into the ocean waiting for the submarine. It would be a huge gamble on their part treading water in the ocean waiting for their rescue from the U.S. Navy. She knew they could remain in the water for at least thirty minutes. There was an hour left of sunlight. After swimming for thirty minutes, they would have to start their swim back to the Shanghai coast and find shelter, dry clothes and some food for the night. That's if they found their way out of the fog swimming in the right direction to the coast.

This was becoming more than a nightmare, it was a spooky alien unfamiliar test of Pilar's mettle. Pilar kept her left hand clinched in a fist while her right hand held tight on the side rail of the wooden boat. Her eyes were searching for the black submarine.

The evil genius was mischievous. The evil genius was as cheerful as Santa Claus.

He found a friend in need. Pilar felt his presence. She could not see his face but knew he was playing with her. The evil genius wanted to catch her off guard and make her a believer. Pilar held true to her religious beliefs: The Father, The Son and The Holy Ghost do exist. If Pilar did not believe in the Trinity, the evil genius could do wicked things and make her suffer. The evil genius is a time traveler. He moves in mysterious ways. He has been around for centuries. This genius can be anywhere, at any time waiting to enter Pilar's mind. The genius was toying with Pilar making her doubt her assignment. Who was the watcher? Where is the submarine? Could the evil genius be controlling events? The evil genius did not hand out subpoenas nor did it want money but his evil was free for the offering. Pilar's mind was stronger than panic. The genius needed to gradually move into her mind since Pilar tossed panic overboard. Its cousins are confusion and conflict. The evil genius wasted no time to practice confusion and conflict in the mind of Pilar. The evil genius used confusion and conflict as a weapon. He wanted to have a hold on her. He was smiling at her. With his warm and gentle touch of this hand, the genius was rubbing her shoulder and softly, so ever softly, whispering into her ear. Asking her to please let me in. The evil genius wanted to foil her assignment. The evil genius demanded to stop Pilar's assignment. The evil genius became frustrated. He did not get his way to enter Pilar's mind. So, he wrapped his long arm on to Pilar's shoulders and whispered into her ear. He let her know he would push the Chinese patrol boat closer to her escaping boat in the fog.

The reason the evil genius chose Pilar not because she was weak and volatile, but he did not like strong attractive women. The evil genius wanted to control her, put her in her place. There was no time limit to his evil. Pilar could not smell his wickedness. She was only aware of the scalpel the evil genius was using trying to slice into her thoughts. The evil genius tried several ways to jolt Pilar. She was strong, maybe too strong for his unpleasantness. The evil genius was not a ghost. The evil genius walked into Pilar's mind when doubt, hesitation or uncertainty appeared. The evil genius realized Pilar was a tense, dedicated and a morally strong woman. He postponed his opus on Pilar. He sat confused sitting on the wooden seat next to Pilar.

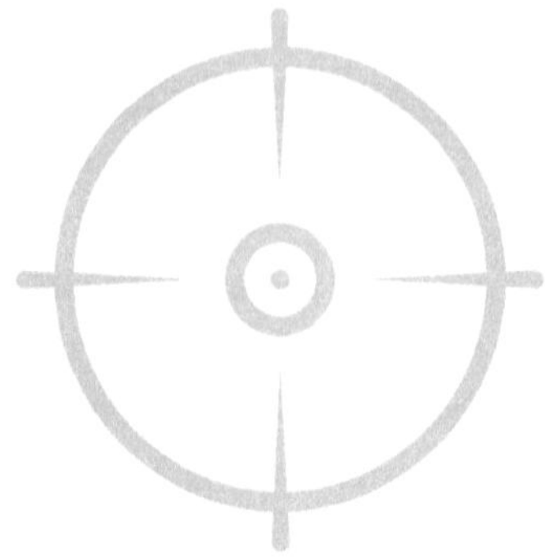

CHAPTER NINETEEN

usty entered their secret satellite department on the second floor of the Alexander Hamilton Foundation. Immediately, he asked the current officer on duty, "How are we doing on our team in Shanghai?" He looked down at his watch. The time was three-thirty in the morning. "Is there any coffee, here?"

"The satellite will only stay on station for about ten minutes. As you can see, there is another boat advancing on our team." Reported the satellite technician. "I checked the weather report for Shanghai. They have fog offshore. It appears there has been some altercation on the dock." He looked at Dusty and pointed to the person who fell into the boat on their large computer screen. "One man has fallen into an empty boat and he seems to be knocked out, because he isn't moving. Maybe, he has been shot? We can't tell. And then we see another person who is laying on the deck. Could he have been shot, too? He isn't moving. He is just lying there. It appears there are several people getting out of the boat to help the person on the dock. The satellite view from above shows the movement on the dock from one hundred feet above the team. We don't have the technology yet to focus any clearer or closer to what we are viewing," remarked Arthur, the senior operator of the satellite operation.

Marie, the other satellite technician, handed Dusty a hot cup of coffee. Looking at the computer screen she commented, "The images we see have a twenty second delay. The electronic images have to feed through the satellite and down to our monitor screen on top of our building. We don't see the images in real time."

Dusty gazed at the satellite screen. He studied both boats' movements in the ocean. "This not good." He turned to ask Arthur, "Has our destroyer arrived and standing in international waters?"

"We can only scan the satellite viewer in a small radius which is about no more than a hundred-yard radius. We can watch our team motor in the fog. As you can see, we have," Arthur counted the number of occupants in the little boat. " four, five, six people in the craft."

"Six people. We should only have Pilar and Ming-Li and Nick in the boat. Who are these other people?"

"I have a feeling, Dusty, that they have picked up a few more people." Marie gazed at his empty coffee mug. She pointed to the coffee pot.

Dusty waltzed over to grab himself a second cup of coffee and returned to view the satellite screen watching the team in the boat. "This is tense watching our team. I guess they are looking for a rendezvous location. Are they close to the pickup point?"

"Very close, sir. Is the submarine to pick them up?" asked Arthur.

"No. We have sent a destroyer who should be in international waters. They will send a zodiac to collect our team. All we do now, is wait and watch."

"I see. By the way, Dusty, we have about one minute of viewing time for this segment. As you know, the satellite will be back online in ninety minutes."

"I'll be in my cubicle downstairs for now. See you both in ninety minutes." As Dusty walked down to his cubicle he said to himself, 'this job does not pay enough money.'

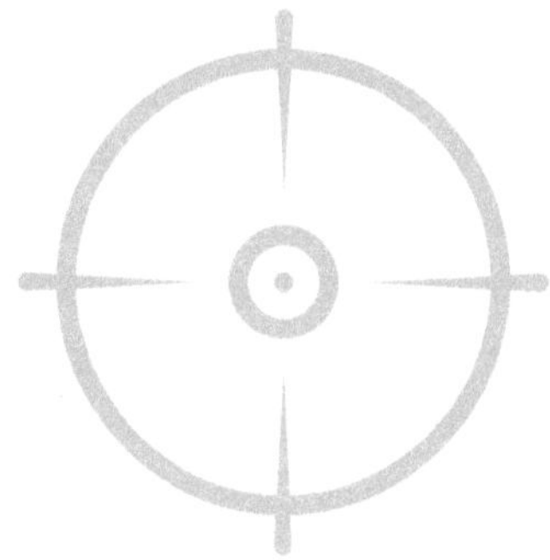

CHAPTER TWENTY

The USS Ingersoll decreased its speed to a crawl and its course is near the shores of Shanghai. The direction of the destroyer is slowly entering the fog bank. As fate would have it, the Ingersoll will fortunately hide in the fog. Connie was familiar with fog from her summer intern work on her uncle's tugboat on Lake Erie. Standing in the wheelhouse peering at the thick fog Chester and Ed glanced at Connie. She remarked to them, "This fog is advantageous to us." She looked at Ed. "You have the wristwatch that will tell you when you reach the rendezvous point, right?"

Ed nodded his head. "Yes."

Connie explained to Chester and Ed, "Fog becomes a visible cloud. Once inside the fog, it can become thick or thin. Fog can become difficult to see through. Fog has tiny water pellets which are suspended in the air near the surface of the land or water. Fog produces precipitation in the form of drizzle. The drizzle occurs when the humidity is at one hundred percent. As we know, navigation becomes dangerous. The fog appears when the weather conditions are highly humid. Sea fog appears near bodies of salt water and becomes water vapor. The thickness of the fog layer is determined by the atmospheric pressure. As the temperature varies, fog can form quickly and then evaporate just as fast. This is called flash fog. Depending on the concentration of the tiny water droplets, visibility inside the fog bank varies from a haze to making you blind which disorients your senses. You might develop fear about which way you are traveling. As I know, fog is different from mist. Fog is much denser; therefore, the fog is massive and heavier than mist. As we see, the fog has more water molecules in the same area of space than mist." She took a sip of her coffee.

"Guys, there are distinct types of fog which are advection fog, freezing fog, radiation fog and valley fog. When warm air slowly moves over a cooler surface, advection fog forms. A scientific name which describes the movement of fluid. The wind becomes fluid. As the moist warm air contacts the cooler surface air, the water vapor compresses to make fog. The radiation fog forms in the evening as heat from the day is absorbed by the surface temperature. The heat is transferred from the soil to the air. Sometimes people call this ground fog and this fog forms at night. In the morning as the sun heats up the air, one sees a burning off of the radiation fog. As one knows, valley fog appears in the valleys of mountains usually in winter. The fog is trapped in the valley which prevents the dense air from escaping. In freezing fog, this fog appears when the liquid fog droplets freeze to the solid surfaces." Connie looked at Chester and Ed, "Clear as mud right, guys?" She offered a grin and took another sip from her coffee mug. She looked at Henry at the helm. "All stop." Since the engines have stopped, one could not feel the vibration from the engines throughout the ship, especially on the decks. "Ed, do you need any help moving the zodiac onto the side of Proud Mary?"

"I don't believe so, Ma'am." Ed turned to Chester. "Shall we turn-two and head on down below to get the zodiac over the side?"

"Of course. You do know, I'm going with you." Chester was serious when he told Ed of his going along with him.

"That's fine." Ed turned to exit the wheelhouse departing for the zodiac.

"Hold up, Ed." Connie quickly stated. She watched Ed stop in his tracks. He turned his head to listen to her. "You'll have about ten to fifteen minutes to locate them and ten to fifteen minutes to return. In a half hour, I will sound the horn every five minutes for you to find us in this fog. Got it?"

Ed looked directly into Connie's eyes. "Yes, Ma'am, I got it." Ed and Chester departed for the unloading of the zodiac. Holding in his hand is the handheld walkie-talkie which he placed in his pocket. Ed glanced at Chester and pointed toward the zodiac. "Chester, take hold of the port and starboard lines at the bow and I'll grab hold of the aft lines. It will be easy to get the zodiac over the side. We just need to get it over the lifelines of Proud Mary." Ed watched Chester easily lift and move the bow of the zodiac over the lifelines and lower the zodiac in the water.

Chester watched Ed calmly lift the aft section with two Honda outboard motors attached to the zodiac over the side. Chester grabbed one of the lines while Ed held the other line lowering the zodiac into the water. "Are we ready to go?"

"Yes, sir. All we need to do is climb down this line into the zodiac and untie the bow and aft lines." Ed climbed over the side and watched Chester do the same. "Chester, if you will, sit in the middle of the zodiac. This will give us balance as we cut through the waves." Ed started both engines. He looked up at Connie and waved. "See you in about thirty minutes." Ed angled the motors away from the ship and pushed away from the side of the ship. They were on their way in the thick fog. Ed cranked the throttles to full speed.

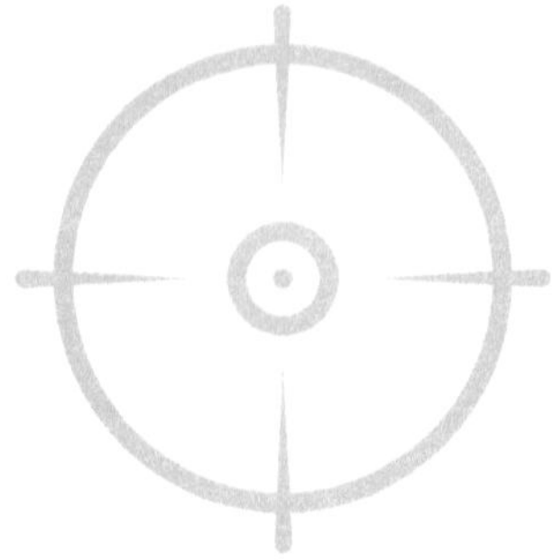

CHAPTER TWENTY-ONE

With the engine off in the twenty-foot boat, the three-foot rolling waves in the East China Sea rocked the boat up and down. They all heard the Chinese patrol boat slowly cruise about fifty feet from them in the dense fog. The patrol boat was crisscrossing their direction trying to locate them. The patrol boat was relentless. Cruising at three to five knots and then shutting off its engine. The patrol boat would glide and listen for voices in the fog. They were in pursuit of possible drug smugglers.

Pilar had a feeling the next time the patrol boat cruised by them they would be caught. She thought maybe the submarine was waiting for the patrol boat to leave the area and then the sub would surface. Their rescue would be moments away. The assignment will be over. Pilar glanced at her watch. It was over an hour from their pickup time of six o'clock. She threw panic, confusion and conflict out of her mind. She was responsible for Ming-Li, her mother, Nick, his girlfriend, Candace and her friend, Margaret. She was not going to drop the ball and fumble.

She understood they were nervous when the patrol boat cruised by. Pilar wondered why the submarine had not surfaced by now, it puzzled her mind. From her naval training, she recognized something went wrong.

Off in the distance, they all turned their heads to the sounds of the motor coming from the patrol boat encroaching toward them. They listened to the patrol boat making waves churning through the water hunting for them through the constant curtain of fog. Pilar thought for sure; they would be caught this time. They were on a collision course with the patrol boat. Pilar whispered, "Everyone, over the side and into the water."

Candace turned around and asked, "Why?"

Pilar saw Margaret as she turned around and questioned her request or was it her command. "Get in the water, now. Once we are in the water, I'll start the engine and head the boat off in the opposite direction from the patrol boat. The Chinese will follow the noise of the engine."

"Are you sure?" asked Nick.

"Yes. I am sure. Nick. Please grab the two oars and place them in the water, too." Pilar pointed to Ming-Li. "Get into the water. You and your mother." She watched as Ming-Li helped her mother climb over the side of the boat and slip into the water. Pilar saw Ming-Li and her mother bob on the water like two wine corks. "Margaret, over the side of the boat. If you get tired of treading water, you can hang on Candace's life vest. Nick, you can hang on the two oars. I'm going to start the engine and turn it away from the patrol boat, so they will follow this boat."

"How long can we do this?" asked Candace.

"We can last about ten minutes."

"So, what happens after ten minutes?" A sudden warm ocean wave entered her mouth. Candace spit out the salty water.

"We will swim back to shore." Commented Pilar. Pilar pulled the ripcord and the Honda engine hummed. She slipped the engine into forward gear. She turned the throttle ever so slightly to give the boat some forward movement and aimed the boat away from them, hence the patrol boat would follow the boat. Pilar slowly slipped overboard. "Let's stay together, all right?"

Candace asked, "How far is it to the shore?"

"Oh, it is about a mile. It would be an easy swim. Nothing to worry about."

A satellite from the Alexander Hamilton Foundation appeared over the site. Dusty stood motionless holding his third cup of coffee viewing the computer screen as it displayed people exiting the escape boat and slipping into the water. Dusty barked, "I don't believe this. They are in the water swimming?"

One of the nameless computer personnel remarked, "If you remember, Dusty, there is fog all around them. They are hiding from the Chinese patrol boat hunting for them."

"Thanks. I forgot about the fog. The fog must be super thick." Dusty took a sip from his coffee cup.

"That would be correct. Otherwise, they would have been captured by now."

"It's a smart move by Pilar getting them into the water and sending their boat the opposite direction away from them. I see the patrol boat following their empty boat. Yeah, it is a brilliant move on her part."

"Is the sub picking them up?"

Dusty steadied his eyes on the computer screen. He answered, "No. No sub is to pick them up. We have a navy destroyer standing by in international waters. They should have sent a zodiac to rescue them."

Dusty set his coffee cup down and folding his arms on his chest as he studied them swimming in the ocean. He asked, "How much time do we have to watch them?"

"About ten more minutes." The computer analyst watched them stationary in the water. He pointed to the screen. "Look! The zodiac is close by." He turned to Dusty. "See it?"

Dusty grit his teeth. His eyes opened wider as he watched the zodiac approach them. "Why don't they pick them up?

"It's the fog. They can't see them in the fog."

"Yeah. Yeah, that's right. They are so close." Remarked Dusty. He remained stationary glued to the computer screen watching the zodiac search for them. "How much time do we have to watch them?"

"The satellite will be on station for about one more minute."

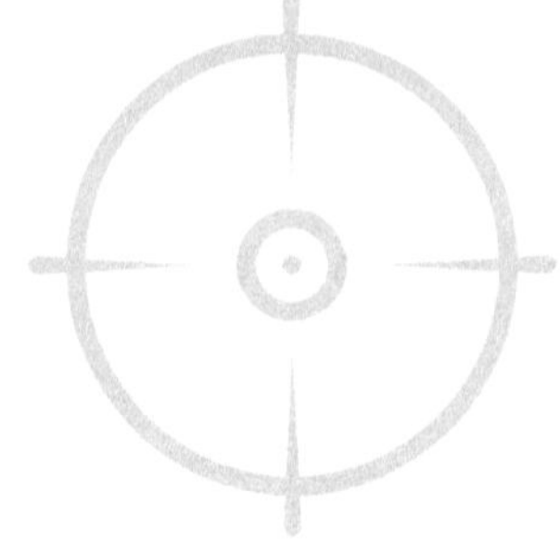

CHAPTER TWENTY-TWO

Pilar heard the Chinese patrol boat motor toward their boat. It felt like the patrol boat was fifty feet from them. The noise from the patrol boat soon vanished. She was pleased her trick worked by sending their empty boat away knowing the patrol boat would be in pursuit. Treading water in the East China Sea was easy for Pilar. Suddenly, she heard a distant man's voice.

"Alexander Hamilton Foundation are you there?" asked Ed from the zodiac. Ed turned off the motors from the zodiac. He was at the correct coordinates for the pickup location. He repeated, "Alexander Hamilton Foundation, are you here?" Ed and Chester listened for a response. Their eyes searching in the fog for them.

Pilar heard the distant voice, again. "We are here." She paused. "We are here!" Pilar slapped the water several times to make some noise to give the distant voice some direction to locate them. She heard the hum of the rescue boat grow louder. It was coming for them. "Over here." Her voice became louder. "Here, we are!" She knew they came from the submarine. She was looking in the approaching direction from the hum of the rescue boat's motor. She did not see them only a surrounding wall of fog. Without warning, the zodiac popped through the sheets of fog. Pilar was not happy or overjoyed to see them, but relieved they were finally saved. The assignment is over. She was going back home to Hawaii.

Pilar looked at the two faces in the zodiac. She squinted her eyes. She thought she saw her husband, Chester. She heard his strong voice.

"Pilar?" Chester paused. His eyes were wide open looking down from the zodiac at her in the water. "What? What are you doing here?"

Ed quickly barked, "Let's get everybody in the zodiac! That patrol boat may have heard us and they might be coming back." Ed set the engine to idle. The ocean lapped against the zodiac. He and Chester lifted Ming-Li and her Mother into the zodiac. Then they lifted Margaret into the zodiac.

Pilar said, "Be careful with Nick. He has a wound on his chest." She watched as Chester and Ed gently pulled Nick up from the water into the boat. They saw his red soaked shirt. She pulled on Candace's life vest dragging her closer to the zodiac. Candace was quickly hoisted into the zodiac by Ed. Pilar raised her arm up and Chester grabbed hold of her hand lifting her up into the zodiac with one pull. "Let's get out of here!" She watched as Ed shifted the lever on the twin Honda engines to forward. Pilar's eyes were fixed on Chester's face. "How did you get here?" Suddenly, they all heard machine gun fire in the distance. Pilar knew the patrol boat must have shot up their empty wooden boat. Ed turned the throttle to increase their speed. "Is the sub close by?" Pilar asked Chester.

"What sub? There is no submarine. We came from Sasebo on a destroyer."

"What?" Pilar was in disbelief. "They said a submarine would pick us up." She watched as Chester shook his head, no. "I don't believe this. If you had not come from Japan to rescue us, we would be swimming back to shore by now." Pilar wanted to kiss Chester but knew it would be inappropriate at this time. "I'm so happy you are here. So, how far is it to the destroyer?"

Chester glanced at his watch. "Oh, about ten more minutes." Chester looked at Ed. "Do you think the patrol boat might be following us?"

Ed responded, "It depends if they turned their engines off to listen for voices or another boat in the area. Let's make it a bad scenario. I would say, yes. They would be following us. We are at full speed now. Hopefully, in about eight minutes we will shut off the engines and listen for Proud Mary's foghorn. Once we hear her horn, we will know which direction to go." Ed saw Chester's fist with a raised thumb signaling an okay.

Pilar, who was dripping wet, sat next to Chester just ahead of Ed, who was steering the zodiac in the direction of the destroyer. Chester's arm lay on his wife's shoulders. The zodiac was bouncing over the three-foot waves like a thrown flat stone skipping over the water. As the zodiac bounced over the waves, Pilar saw Candace holding Nick in her lap. Margaret was sitting next to Nick and holding on to the seat from the recoiling zodiac. Pilar watched Ming-Li and her mother holding on to their seats getting sprayed from the vaulting bow over the waves of the zodiac. Pilar's mind was at rest. She did not have to think about her responsibility to get Ming-Li out of Shanghai. She accomplished her task. She felt the zodiac slow down and heard the foghorn from the destroyer. The zodiac made a course change toward the destroyer. Ed cranked the throttle to flank speed. The zodiac lunged ahead and was again bouncing over the waves. Pilar sat quietly looking ahead with her left hand holding on to the seat and her right hand tightly holding on to Chester's wrist. She was away from the friction of the assignment. She felt safe.

The gray destroyer appeared out of the fog. Ed slowed the zodiac and drifted to the port side of the ship. Two sailors appeared lowering down lines to secure the zodiac to the hull of the ship. Two ladders were set resting on the hull. A line was placed around Ming-Li as she climbed up the ladder to the deck. She watched as her mother climbed up the ladder. Margaret and Candace climbed up the ladder with ease. Nick slowly moved up the ladder to the deck. Pilar grabbed hold of the rungs of the ladder climbing up the ladder to the main deck. Last to follow were Chester and Ed. Chester and Ed slowly hoisted the zodiac aboard the ship.

Connie motioned to the new arrivals to follow the two sailors below to the mess deck. Connie said, "Make sure they get blankets and some hot soup and sandwiches, all right guys?" She watched as the two sailors nodded, yes. "And don't forget to get them dry shirts and pants."

Ming-Li started to follow the two sailors but stopped and turned back toward Pilar. She took off her wet life vest and placed it on the gray steel deck. Ming-Li helped her mother off with her life vest. Ming -Li looked up at the mast of the destroyer gazing at the limp American flag. She turned and walked back to Pilar. She managed to offer a small grin. "Thank you, Pilar." She grabbed hold of Pilar and hugged her with both arms. She released her warm hug and accompanied her mother below following the sailors.

Nick helped Candace off with her life vest placing the vest on the deck. He could see her ocean-soaked shirt sealed around both of her large breasts revealing her hard nipples. "Let's get below and warm up." He listened to Ed who told him to get below. Nick kicked off his wet shoes and left them on the deck.

Candace pulled off her shoes and socks. She helped Nick pull off his wet socks and placed them on the deck. "This is a big boat."

As he looked at Nick, Ed remarked, "I can give you a penicillin shot in case there is an infection. Also, I'll numb your chest area and stich you up."

Margaret walked behind Candace and Nick. She also kicked off her socks and shoes leaving them on the deck. She kept looking around the ship. She could not believe she was aboard an American destroyer.

Pilar watched Ed and Chester secure the zodiac to the deck. She turned to walk with Margaret. "Pretty big ship, huh?"

"My gosh. I never realized this type of ship was so huge." Remarked Margaret. "Let's get below to get some chow and dry clothes."

Unexpectedly, they all heard the motor of the Chinese patrol boat roaring toward them. "I'm sure they heard our foghorn." Connie snapped. "Ed, get the zodiac secured! We are getting out of here, pronto!" She ran from the deck up the ladder to the bridge. "Engine room, give us flank speed, now!" Connie heard an aye, aye from the Engine room. "Henry, set the course to Sasebo, Japan. Let's get out of here!" The USS Ingersoll lunged forward. The interior steel decks of the ship started to vibrate. Within two minutes the destroyer was out of the fog bank.

Chester climbed up the ladder to the bridge. "Connie, can I get you some coffee?"

"Sure, that would be nice. Oh, and bring a cup for Henry, too, Okay?"

As Chester turned to exit the bridge he said, "No problem." Chester glided below into the mess deck and saw that everyone had blankets around them and they were warming up with hot soup and cold ham and cheese sandwiches. He sat down next to Pilar. "How did you?" He paused. "Why didn't you call me about this assignment?" He offered a small smile.

Pilar finished her sandwich. "Well, my love. It's like this," She took a sip of her soup. "Admiral Mahone asked me if I could help the Alexander Hamilton Foundation on this easy assignment getting Ming-Li out of Shanghai. That I was a perfect fit for a Pacific Asian to get her out of China. The mission was top secret. She believed this would be an easy assignment. But I think there was a leak because someone was following us. This guy pulled a gun on us at the boat dock. If it hadn't been for Nick's quick thinking and knocking this guy off balance with a boat oar. We would not be here. The guy tripped backwards off the wooden pier and fell back into the moored boat across from our boat. His reflex was to grab something. Well, he was holding a gun and he pulled the trigger. The bullet hit Nick just grazing his chest. The guy fell into the boat hitting his head. I jumped out of our boat and took his sunglasses off to look at his face. I did not recognize him, but I took his gun. I was told not to talk to anyone about this mission. I was also told a submarine would pick us up." She stared at Chester's face.

"My gosh. This sounds like a spy movie."

"If it wasn't for Nick's girlfriend, Candace, she helped us get away moving throughout the streets of Shanghai, again, I don't think we would have made it. This guy kept following us."

Chester saw one of the sailors appear and say they have dry clothes for everyone. "Well, you are safe now, my love." His arm wrapped around her shoulders and he kissed her forehead.

"Thank you. I just want to push this out of my mind." Pilar took a deep breath. "I am simply exhausted." She stood up and walked to get some dry clothes.

Candace pulled from her pocket her soaked visa. "Oh, no." She looked at Pilar.

"Hand it to me, I'll gently open it and the air will dry the visa. Let's get some dry clothes."

Chester watched all of them exit the mess deck to get some dry clothes. He grabbed two coffee mugs and filled them with hot coffee.

Over the loudspeaker, Connie called, "Captain Marshall, to the bridge."

Chester thought Connie must need the coffee in a hurry. He entered the bridge handing the coffee mugs to Connie and Henry, the helmsman.

"Thanks for the coffee. We got trouble." Connie handed Chester her night binoculars and pointed off her port quarter. "I think someone is following us."

Chester took hold of the binoculars. "Yeah. I see some lights. It doesn't seem the lights of a fishing boat, but of a warship." He handed the binoculars back to Connie. "We are cruising at flank speed, right?"

Connie looked at Chester, "Yes, sir." She looked through the glasses again asking, "Could you tell the distance they are at?"

"I'd say, oh, about a mile or two away from us."

"Could you tell their hull number or their colors,?"

"No, I could not." Chester replied.

"Bridge, this is the engine room."

"What is the problem?" Connie asked.

"We have a problem with the carburetor. We are losing power. Seems the diesel fuel clogged up the jets in the carburetor. When we last refueled from the oiler, we probably received the dregs from the bottom of their diesel fuel supply. We need to clean it, then we can resume our high rpm. We have to stop the engine to clean the carburetor."

"Engine room, we have people following us."

"The carburetor is starving for fuel. We need to clean it, now."

"Understood. How long will this take?"

"Oh, about twenty minutes."

"Make it fast. We are on someone's radar and we need to get out of here," replied Connie. She could see the fast-approaching vessel. The Chinese patrol boat boomed something in Chinese over their loudspeaker. Connie looked at Chester. "Do you know what they are saying?"

Chester shook his head no and took hold of the bridge's 1MC microphone and said, "Lieutenant Commander Marshall to the bridge." He commented to Connie, "Pilar speaks fluent Mandarin. She'll tell us what they are asking."

The engines have stopped. The USS Ingersoll was dead in the water. While the two sailors in the engine room worked on the engineering problem, they were quiet and as they pulled off the carburetor and cleaned it. The Chinese patrol boat approached the USS Ingersoll. The patrol boat was one hundred yards off the ship's port side. They boomed again in Mandarin.

Pilar walked into the wheelhouse and looked at the Chinese patrol boat with their spotlight focused on the destroyer.

Connie asked, "Commander, do you know what they are saying?"

"They want to board us."

"We are in international waters. There is no way they are boarding us. Tell them we are in international waters and the answer is no," barked Connie.

Chester said, "I believe they have communicated to one of their big brothers to visit us. We need to get out of here. I'm sure one of the Chinese destroyers will be showing up soon."

Connie said, "We are in international waters."

Pilar commented looking at Connie, "They don't care. This is their pond and we are in violation according to them."

"No way, are the Chinese coming aboard my ship!" Connie turned to her helmsman. "Henry, shine Proud Mary's spotlight on that patrol boat, please."

All of a sudden the USS Ingersoll's flood of bright spotlight bloomed on the Chinese patrol boat. The destroyers spotlight was four times brighter than the spotlight from the patrol boat. "Engine room, Bridge, where do we sit on the carburetor?"

"We just got it off to clean. You keep interrupting us and it will take longer to clean."

Connie shook her head rolling her eyes as she hung up the 1MC microphone. She accompanied Chester to the outside catwalk peering at the patrol boat.

Ming-Li climbed the ladder to the bridge looking for Pilar. She looked at the light shown on the patrol boat. "Pilar, why is the patrol boat shining its spotlight on this ship and why aren't we moving away?"

Pilar took hold of Ming-Li's arm to calm her down. "Well, the patrol boat that was looking for us followed the noise from the zodiac that brought us here. Now, they want to come aboard."

"Oh no. They must not come aboard."

Pilar saw her frightened face. "They are not coming aboard. We are in international waters. Commander Resnis will not allow them to board us. The sailors in the engine room are repairing the engine. We will be underway shortly."

"Pilar what did you do in the navy?"

Pilar glanced away for a moment and then responded to Ming-Li. "Have you ever read 'The Pentagon Papers' book, which came out it the seventies?"

"Yes, I read the book about ten years ago. Why?"

"Well, the book covered some highly sensitive areas of information which people like me, who work in intelligence use every day."

"Yes, I see. So, I can tell you this information on what I do."

"What information, Ming-Li?"

"I am head of the Cyber Department in Shanghai, in fact all of China. I listened to the Russian President Putin and our Chinese President Xi discuss what they are going to do to the western nations. It will be very ugly."

"What do you mean, ugly?"

"In all good consciousness and good manners, I cannot stand by and let them do this mean application to the western nations."

"I know you are escaping to the west, which is fine, but what do you mean by this terrible application to the west?"

"Believe me, I am not kidding you."

"I believe you, Ming-Li."

"I listened to the two of them discussing military movements into Ukraine and then into Romania and into Poland, Finland and Latvia. What is the United States going to do? Simultaneously, China will move its military to take over Taiwan.

Again, they know the United States will do nothing. What could they do? Initiate financial restrictions? Then this evil force will ask North Korea to move into Seoul, South Korea with their military. It will be a bloody mess, as well as a world monetary disaster. The final push by China will be to squeeze Japan like Japan squeezed China during World War Two."

"And you heard all this from Putin and Xi?"

Ming-Li slowly motioned her head, yes. Her black eyes were locked on Pilar's face. "Yes, Pilar. I listened to their conversation. I have their voices locked in a virtual space on the internet. I know the key to unlock their voices. The strongest country on this planet will do nothing. America will only shout their protests in the United Nations for the rest of the nations to hear." She paused. "What is United Kingdom, France or Germany going to do? Nothing." Ming-Li took hold of Pilar's arm stressing the need for her to listen. "These two guys are serious, Pilar. I could not stand by and do nothing. The western nations need to know what Putin and Xi are thinking. These two people do not want peace. They are acting like Stalin and Mao Tse -Tung and what these two dictators accomplished in the fifties. They want control. They hate the west. As far as I am concerned, they have mental problems. These two leaders are unbalanced. The Chinese people and the Russian people are peaceful peoples, but these two leaders are crazy. They are mentally uneven. I cannot over stress the need in which your American President needs to listen to their conversation. No one else knows I have a recording of their conversation. I have the recording in Cypher Space." Ming-Li retracted her arm from Pilar and bowed her head for a moment. She raised her head and gazed up at Pilar. "Pilar, this is why I am leaving China. You have to take me to America. Do you understand?"

"Yes, Ming-Li. I understand." She saw the flood of tears from Ming-Li's eyes as they began to cascade down her cheeks. Pilar could see Ming-Li was drenched in worry.

"We need to rapidly get out of this situation at sea and get me to America. Thank you, Pilar for getting me to this point." Ming-Li grit her teeth and said, " I cannot over stress, we need to get away! We have a quantum computer, which I have developed. It is much faster than your CIA or NSA computers."

Pilar asked, "What is a quantum computer?"

Ming-Li explained. "Quantum computers manipulate quantum physics which store information or data. On your everyday computer, it uses zeros and ones to encode the information in a binary form called bits, whereas a quantum computer uses a unit of memory as a qubit. These qubits use an electron which this property becomes a quantum entanglement to make a long story short a few hundred entanglement qubits can, how can I explain this?" She paused and looked away and turned her head back to Pilar. "These hundred entanglements can understand that there are more numbers than atoms in the universe. This system obeys the Church-Turing thesis, which is a convoluted theory."

"Wow. This is all news to me."

"What this system can do is shut down electricity in anything for that matter. This computer can shut down electricity grids for cities. We have the coded information on where to shut down electricity in Seattle, Los Angeles, Chicago and Houston, Texas. This new electric war China is planning to use against the United States and then to various counties in Europe. This is the information we have recorded. This is why I am escaping from China. This evilness is wrong." Ming-Li clinched her fists. " Your government needs to know about this mean plan they have stored and ready to implement. Pilar, I need to get to America. I want to live to be forty-eight. You see China does not need to send assassins to America, only to cut off the use of electricity to bring America to its knees. Without the use of electricity, your people will not be able to pump gasoline into their cars. The electricity will be cut off. The grocery stores' food will rot because there will be no refrigeration. There will be panic. You will not be able to get your money out of the bank since there will be no electricity. There will be limited communication since there will be no television or phone service. These two leaders are evil. Do you understand me!"

Pilar saw the seriousness on the face of Ming-Li. "Chester, Commander Resnis, we need to get out of here. We need to get Ming-Li to safety."

Connie heard Pilar and walked into the wheelhouse and picked up the 1MC microphone. "Engine room, where do we sit?"

"All most done, Commander. Just a few more minutes, we'll be ready to move like lightening," replied the engineman. "We'll let you know."

"Roger."

Pilar asked Ming-Li to go below to get some more food. Pilar watched her depart the bridge and turned to Chester and Connie. "We need to get out of here fast."

Connie said, "Yes, we know. I certainly don't like sitting here like a duck in their pond, but we are in international waters. "

Pilar looked down at the steel deck. She was still swimming in the river of friction. Pilar slowly raised her head. She explained why they needed to rapidly get away. "Well, Ming-li has designed a supercomputer which can somehow sneak into our electrical base in various cities and turn off the electrical power to these cities. Meaning they, the Chinese government, can do what they want in the world while the United States tries to figure out how to restore electrical power. She also heard Putin and Xi discussing what they might do to grab more territory. Ming-Li has their conversations on tape hidden somewhere in the supercomputer. She wants to have our President listen to this powerful information. When she found this information of what these evil two leaders want to do, this is when she decided to defect to our side."

"I see your point. Engine room, how about it? Do we have power?" asked an anxious skipper.

"Bridge, port watch. We have sighted some oncoming lights advancing straight toward us."

Connie grabbed the 1MC. "Tell me it's a cruise ship. Right?"

"I don't think so, Commander," reported the port watch.

"Tell me what you see."

"On the horizon, I see three lights on their mast."

Connie spoke into the 1MC with a little more of her naval tone. "Engine room, we need power. We have visitors, who will soon be arriving here. Got it!" She heard silence. She turned to her helmsman and said, "Turn off the spotlight." Then she turned looking at Chester. "Captain, I don't like sitting here, helpless."

"Bridge, I think our bogey fired a shot. I saw a flash of light."

All of a sudden, they heard an eerie sound rip through the sky and then a huge plash of water erupted about one hundred yards just north away from the USS Ingersoll. The Chinese destroyer sent a calling card notifying the intruder to leave. Connie called Mike the sharpshooter to the bridge. She asked him to get his girlfriend and take out the patrol boat's spotlight. "Mike, the patrol boat's spotlight is giving the Chinese an eye on us. Can you do it with one shot?"

Looking at Connie, Mike offered a small grin and winked his eye. "I sure can, Skipper." He saw a big smile on her face. He turned to leave the darkened interior of the bridge and skipped on down to the weapons locker. Mike was a second- class petty officer in charge of the weapons on the ship. He was raised in Colorado. He was taught by his grandfather how to shoot a rifle.

Chester asked Connie, "Who is his girlfriend?"

"Oh, yeah. It's Mike's personal Benelli Lupo bolt-action rifle with a scope. He is an expert shooter. With his rifle, he can do the job." Connie nodded her head, yes.

Moments later, Mike returned to the bridge with his girlfriend. He glanced at Captain Marshall. He offered to show his rifle to the captain. "Isn't she a beauty?" From the patrol boat's light beaming on the bridge of the Ingersoll, Mike handed his girlfriend to Captain Marshall.

"Nice walnut finish on your rifle," commented Chester as he handed the rifle back to Mike.

"Thanks, Captain Marshall. Yep, She can take a bear or a deer out at two hundred yards." Mike looked at Connie as he placed one shell into the Benelli. I brought an extra shell in case I miss." Mike grinned and whispered, "I won't miss." Mike walked out from the interior of the bridge to the catwalk peering at the patrol boat's spotlight. He carefully raised the Benelli rifle to his shoulder and slowly leaned his head forward having his cheek rest next to the walnut stock, so his right eye could stare into the scope viewing the spotlight. To steady his girlfriend, Mike leaned against the metal rail. He wrapped his left arm around the sling of the rifle and with his hand, he securely held the walnut barrel. He rotated his aim from the white-hot light of the Chinese patrol boat's spotlight to the bridge of the patrol boat and observed several Chinese sailors. "I see several Chinese sailors, which I could take out, skipper."

Connie quickly said, "No, Mike. Just the spotlight."

"Aye, aye, skipper." The Ingersoll gently rocked in the ocean. Mike was timing the rocking of the Ingersoll as the Chinese patrol boat rocked back and forth, too. It took several minutes to have both ships rock in the ocean simultaneously in order to take the shot. Mike held his breath. He was calm. There was no wind to challenge his shot. He closed his left eye. His right eye blinked and focused on the spotlight. His right index finger touched the trigger of the Benelli. His aim was spot-on the spotlight. He held his breath. Mike easily squeezed the trigger. On the bridge of the USS Ingersoll, they heard the puff from the rifle. In a few seconds, the Chinese spotlight went black. Mike turned to look at Connie. "Done." He asked, "Do you need anything else from my girlfriend?" He offered a small grin.

"Thank you , Mike and many thanks to your girlfriend." Connie patted Mike on his shoulder. As she picked up the 1MC microphone to talk to the engine room, she watched Mike depart the bridge. "Engine room, bridge. Where do we sit on the engine?"

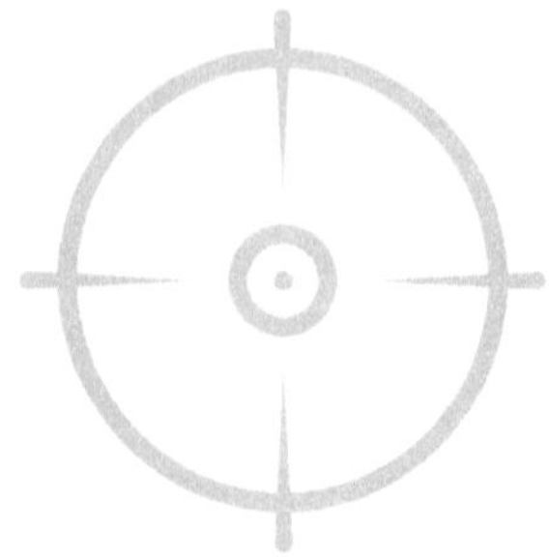

CHAPTER TWENTY-THREE

The satellite took ninety minutes to circumnavigate the globe. The satellite technician, Marie, adjusted the night view which took several minutes for the computer screen to show the destroyer sitting stationary in the ocean. The technician looked at Dusty. "I wonder why the ship isn't moving?"

"I trust this is our ship which picked up our guest?" asked Dusty.

"Oh, yes. It is our ship. If you look a little closer at the mast. You can just make out our flag showing the stars and stripes."

Dusty leaned a little closer to the computer screen. "Yeah. I can see it, now." Dusty glanced at the technician. "Can you expand the view? I want to see if there might be another ship in the area." He watched Marie change the dial. In several minutes, the computer screen doubled in size. He saw another ship advancing toward the stationary ship. "It is a Chinese destroyer advancing on our destroyer." Dusty folded his arms on his chest. "This doesn't look good. What is that splash of white stuff near our destroyer?" He turned his head looking at Marie. "Could it be the Chinese is firing on our destroyer?" He saw Marie nod her head, yes.

CHINESE DESTROYER TYPE 051 LUDA-II CLASS DDG-105 *JINAN*

https://sinodefence.wordpress.com/2017/05/16/type-051-luda-class-destroyer

Dusty pointed at the computer screen. "Over to the left of our destroyer, I see remains of an outline of a wooden boat floating in the ocean. I don't see anyone near the sunken boat. I wonder if the Chinese patrol boat sunk the boat? I'm sure our destroyer picked up our guest with their zodiac." He looked at the satellite tech and said, "I'll be right back." Dusty walked out of the secured satellite room and down to his desk in his cubicle. He dialed Admiral Mahone. He looked at his watch. It read a little after five in the morning. He dialed her number at the naval base in Hawaii knowing she would not be in, but he would leave a voice mail message, anyway.

"Admiral Mahone, may I help you?"

A surprised Dusty answered back. "Morning Admiral. I did not think you'd be in this early. I was going to leave you a voice message."

"We work twenty-four hours a day." She was direct in her response to Dusty.

Dusty commented, "Admiral, we are looking at our destroyer sitting off the coast of Shanghai via our satellite. There is a Chinese war ship which fired a shot at our ship."

"What?"

"It looks as if there is a battle between our ship and the Chinese ship. What can we do?"

"Well, we can't get our jets to the location. It would take too long for them to fly there. There are no other ships in the area." Admiral Mahone looked up at her assistant, Commander Paula Berger, who popped her head into the office.

"Ma'am, the USS North Carolina just hailed us. They are on station watching the Ingersoll."

"Perfect!" shouted Janis. "Paula, send a flash message to the North Carolina and instruct them to assist the Ingersoll in any way they can."

"Aye, aye." Paula turned and ran down the hall to the operations center.

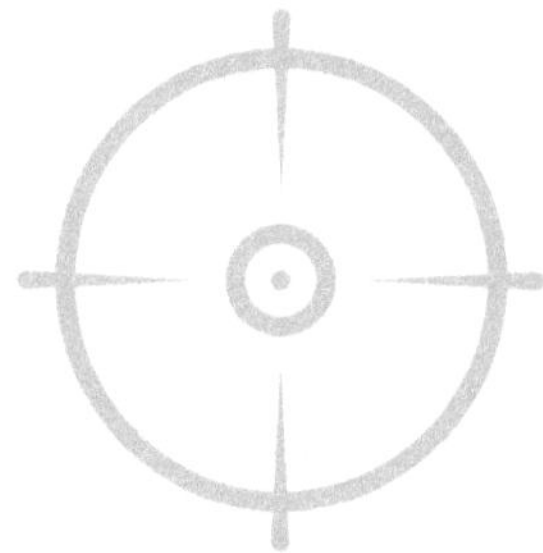

CHAPTER TWENTY-FOUR

The engine room immediately called the bridge where Connie was anxiously waiting for their reply. "We got the turbines working again, Skipper!"

"Thank you, guys." Connie barked. "All ahead, flank!" The Ingersoll lunged forward. The ship rapidly moved ahead from a stationary position. She looked at Chester, "Good to feel the vibration underneath your feet, huh?"

"I'm glad we are moving. We can finally get out of here,'" remarked Chester as he peered at the running lights of the distant Chinese destroyer.

Connie and Chester heard the incoming shell closing in on the Ingersoll. "Henry, turn the ship to the right, now!" Connie looked at Chester, "I hope we miss their salvo aiming in on us." She watched as Henry began to turn the wheel and head to a new course.

As the Ingersoll moved getting out of harm's way, the Chinese destroyer fired another salvo. The salvo was to miss the Ingersoll by fifty yards. It was only a warning for the American destroyer to get out of their backyard. Little did anyone know the Ingersoll was about to be hit. The incoming Chinese shell was on a collision course with the bow of the Ingersoll. Unfortunately, the Ingersoll moved right into the path of the approaching shell. The super-sonic advancing shell was going to crash on the deck of the American destroyer. The Chinese shell smashed into the front gun of the Ingersoll ripping it to a mangled mess. The ripped-up pieces of metal flew up and into the bridge of the Ingersoll. The flying pieces of metal tore into the glass and then blew into the wheelhouse where Chester, Connie and Henry were standing. The sudden blast knocked Chester back to the deck. The concussion threw Connie back to the bulkhead knocking her unconscious. Henry was hit with flying metal and glass shards as he flew back to the bulkhead of the wheelhouse and knocking him down hard to the deck. The Ingersoll kept moving forward at flank speed.

Pilar heard the shell hit the bow of the Ingersoll. She ran from the mess deck down the companion way and up the ladder to the bridge. As she reached the top of the ladder, she saw Connie lying motionless on the deck. Pilar thought a typhoon had hit the bridge. There was electrical wires dangling from the overhead ceiling. The front windows of the bridge were blown out and into the wheelhouse. There was broken glass shards lying everywhere. She heard Henry moaning as he lay on the deck. Pilar watched her husband, Chester as he slowly and quietly moved struggling to get up on his feet. She knew he was stunned. Pilar moved behind the steering wheel of the ship and turned the ship to the right. She picked up the 1MC microphone and told the engine room to bring the engines to an idle. She heard the radioman appear on the ladder. Bruce could not believe his eyes.

Pilar told him. "Get a blanket for Connie."

"Is she?" asked Bruce, the radioman.

"Hopefully, not. Feel the pulse on her neck with your hand."

"I don't feel anything." Answered Bruce.

"Press harder on her neck."

"I got a pulse," Bruce remarked as he looked at Pilar.

" Get two blankets, Now! And tell weapons to load the rear gun and fire at the Chinese destroyer." She watched as he quickly climbed down the ladder. She turned her attention to her husband who was leaning against the chart table.

"Honey, how are you feeling?

Chester looked at his wife, "I'm just a little stunned."

Pilar watched as Chester gently wiped away the blood from his face with is short-sleeved khaki shirt. Chester did not have time to duck and avoid the blast as the glass from the windows of the bridge blew with lightning speed into his face.

Chester was slowly coming around to reality. He asked, "Are we going to fire with our aft gun at the Chinese?"

"Yes."

"When you have time, tell the radioman to send a flash message to Cincpacflt that we are under fire and give our coordinates, too."

"Of course. She watched Chester shake his head trying to get some conscious traction from the hit.

They both heard another shell racing toward the Ingersoll. The splash from the shell landed one hundred feet away from the hull of the Ingersoll's aft port side.

"Chester, their shells are getting closer."

The sonarman appeared on the ladder. His mouth was wide open as he took in the reality of a typhoon which hit the bridge. "Ah."

Pilar looked at him, "What is it?"

"Yeah, there is a blip on the sonar screen."

"Where is it coming from? The north, south, east or west?"

His wide searching eyes were still dissecting the horror. As he gazed at his skipper. "How is Commander Resnis?"

"She is alive. Someone went to get a blanket for her and Henry. Now, Sailor, where on your screen is the blip coming from?

"Oh, yeah. From the east."

All of sudden there was a loud boom from the rear gun of the Ingersoll. Keep us advised on the blip, All right?"

"Yes, Ma'am." He climbed down the ladder and disappeared.

Chester and Pilar watched as the Ingersoll's shell splashed about one hundred feet away from the Chinese destroyer. They waited for another salvo hoping the next shot would hit the Chinese bridge. They heard another blast from the Ingersoll's rear gun. They saw a muzzle flash from the Chinese destroyer. The Ingersoll's shell hit the bridge of the Chinese destroyer. Suddenly, the Chinese shell blasted into the portside hull of the Ingersoll. It was right at the water line. The Ingersoll was taking on gallons of sea water. The Ingersoll rocked back and forth.

Pilar asked Chester, "Are you feeling all right that you can you take the conn?"

"I'm going below to see what happened."

"I'm fading in and out, but I can take the conn." Chester patted his face with his sleeve. The blood on his cheeks began to clot. "Go see what happened below."

She wanted to kiss and hug him, but there was no time. Pilar climbed down the ladder. As she turned to head down the companionway hall, she saw one of the sailors carrying two blankets. He was ready to climb the ladder. "I'm headed aft toward the engine room. Be sure to cover Connie and Henry with the blankets." Pilar climbed down two more ladders to get to the port side and view what hit the Ingersoll. As she opened the hatch, she saw a huge garage sized hole which ripped open the steel hull from the shell launched by the Chinese destroyer. The ocean was pouring into the Ingersoll like water flowing over Niagara Falls. Pilar tried to close the hatch but the force of the oncoming flow of ocean water was too powerful. By the time she realized she could not secure the hatch, water was flowing over the two-foot-high knee knockers of the metal doorway hatch. She quickly turned around and headed down the hallway and secured the hatch and then ran to the starboard side of the ship to go around and see if water was pouring into the engine room. She opened the hatch to the engine room. She saw the blown-out bulkhead. There was no way to secure the engine room from the ocean pouring in. She saw the two sailors trying to stop the flow of water streaming into the engine room. They were standing in knee deep water. "You guys, okay?" She watched an effortless battle. Pilar knew they could not stop the flow of the ocean gushing into the engine room. "Give it up, guys. Shut down the engines."

Both sailors looked at Pilar as if to say, 'we can stop the flow of water.' One of the sailors realized Pilar was right. The water in the engine room was now waist deep.

"Guys, you did the best you could do. It's time to secure the hatch and get topside, all right? Besides, the electricity was to be cut off soon and you both will be in the dark. It is time to leave."

Both sailors were exhausted from trying to stop the water rushing in the engine room. They agreed with Pilar, it was time to quit and get out of the flooded compartment. They heard another blast from the Ingersoll's rear gun. They watched Pilar depart the engine room.

"Guys, get to the main deck. I'm headed to the bridge." Pilar raced down the hallway and up the ladder to the bridge. She saw the blankets on Connie and Henry. She looked at Chester. "Did we knock out the Chinese destroyer?"

"Good to have you back, my dolphin." Chester picked up the binoculars which were laying on the deck. He offered the binoculars to Pilar. "Take a look. Yes, the last shot took out their rudder. As you can see, the Ingersoll's few shots smashed into their bridge and we hit their hull at the waterline. They are taking on water." Chester turned to Pilar. "How does it look below?"

Pilar peered through the binoculars and said, "We are dead in the water. Their shell hit us below the waterline, too. The engine room is flooded. The shell hit the bulkhead supporting the engine room and the adjacent compartment. There is no way to save the ship. The electricity will be out soon." She handed the binoculars back to Chester. "Now, I'm worried when the rest of the Chinese navy will show up." Her eyes pulled away from viewing the Chinese destroyer as she looked at Chester. "Did we get our SOS off to Cincpacflt?"

"I hope so."

"This is turning into one giant nightmare, which does not end." Pilar stopped mid-sentence. " I'm tired of this!" She slammed her fist on the chart table. She glanced down at Connie and Henry laying on the deck. "No one is coming to rescue us. I'm sure the Chinese navy will show up on the horizon when the sun comes up." Pilar saw one of the ship's sailor climb up the ladder. "Could you get two stokes stretchers for your skipper and Henry? We need to get them on to the main deck. And tell everyone to get to the main deck." She watched the sailor nod his head, yes, as he climbed down the ladder.

The evil genius was one step behind her. He missed talking to her. He loved her soft but strong voice. She was perfect to mold into his evil world. He followed her to the Ingersoll. He was sure he could trap her and keep her. The evil genius needed this attractive woman. He knew there were others he could have grabbed hold of, but Pilar was a challenge. He wasn't going to give up on her. There was one problem for the evil genius. He was afraid of her husband, Captain Marshall. When Captain Marshall was near Pilar, the evil genius lost his wicked power.

Chester watched his wife who was full of rage. It was his turn to calm her down. In his calming and low toned voice, he said, "Pilar, we are not licked yet. Have a little faith."

She turned with angry eyes and looked at Chester and in a stronger tone said, "Faith, in what? Look at this ship. Look what the Chinese did to us. We are dead in the water. What can we do, now, but wait to be captured by the Chinese?"

Chester knew when you lose her head from anger, your reasoning power vanishes. This was a true learning point for Chester who needed to walk his wife into calmer waters for her to listen to his reasoning. His sharp blue eyes locked onto Pilar's face. "Pilar, I'm asking you to listen to me for a moment."

"What!" She barked.

Chester knew she was full of anger. "Pilar, all this happened for a reason. You accomplished your mission. The sub did not show up; however, we were called into this complexity. The Chinese want us out of their backyard. The skipper of the Ingersoll is knocked out. I'm sure this destroyer will sink. The pressure of command is on your shoulders. I'm still fading in and out; therefore, you are in command. You have to think about all of us. It is okay to show anger, but not in front of the crew. They see you become extremely angry and they get nervous. Pilar, you are doing just fine. You have the strength and the willpower to move us forward. Do you understand what I am saying?"

"Yes, I understand what you are saying." Pilar paused looking into his forceful eyes and said, "Chester, I want out of this mess."

"I know you do." Chester offered a half smile to his wife.

She recognized his warm smile and replied, "Thank you, Captain Marshall for your comments and keeping me squared away." She wanted to hug and kiss him. She heard one of Ingersoll's sailors call up from the deck below.

"Commander. There is a sub off our starboard side." Ed pointed to the submarine. "Look!"

Pilar looked into the distance and saw the black sub in plain sight. The morning sun was beginning to show its ray of light on the horizon. "That sub better be ours." She watched as the sub gained buoyance. The sub was about one hundred yards away.

USS North Carolina (SSN-777) **185-033.JPGPhoto By: Mass Communication Specialist 2nd Class Brian G. Reynolds** Csp.navy.mil. *This photograph is considered public domain and has been cleared for release.*

Ed appeared at the ladder and looked up at Pilar standing on the bridge. "It is, Commander. Should we get the zodiac lowered?"

"Yes, Ed. Do it now." Pilar for a moment, froze and peered into his serious brown eyes. "And thank you, Ed, for your help." She saw him head off to get the zodiac over the side. She turned and watched her husband walk to the ladder. "Do you need help getting down the ladder?"

"Thanks for asking. I'll see you on the main deck."

Pilar looked at the sun just peering over the horizon. She gazed at the Chinese destroyer sitting quietly about two hundred yards north. Pilar kneeled down to see if Connie was conscious. She watched as she saw Connie slowly awaken.

"How are you doing Commander?"

"Like I've been hit by a truck. How is my ship?" Her eyes widly looked at Pilar.

Pilar responded, "Your sailors knocked out the Chinese destroyer. We have one of our subs alongside us. They are going to take us out of here. I'm going to ask the sub to tow the Ingersoll out to sea. She has taken a lot of water from the Chinese shells. We cannot stop the water from pouring into the ship."

"I see. I know she is in capable hands with you at the helm." Connie offered a partial smile.

"Oh, they are ready to cart you down to the zodiac and off to the sub. See you later, Connie."

In a few minutes, the zodiac was loaded with passengers. The zodiac buzzed from the Ingersoll to the waiting sub which was about fifty to seventy-five yards away. Pilar grabbed one of the ship's sailors and asked if they had a line which they could secure to the bow and have the sub tow the Ingersoll out to sea. The Ingersoll was sinking. She was listing at ten degrees to port. The sailor responded to her request and in a few minutes he came back dragging a two hundred-foot one inch hemp line to the main deck. Pilar mentioned to the sailor and make sure you tie the line securely to the bow and throw the rest of the line over the starboard side.

Pilar stood on the deck of the Ingersoll with her eyes glaring at the submarine.

Asking herself, why didn't the sub pick us up at the rendezvous point instead of the destroyer, Ingersoll? She knew if Chester did not get the call to come pick her up, they would be swimming back to the shoreline of Shanghai or the Chinese would have captured them. Pilar grit her teeth, placed her hands inside her pants pockets and deeply inhaled several times as she stood watching the zodiac motor back from the sub to the Ingersoll to pick up the remaining crew. She felt this covert adventure was rushed. There was not enough time to plan for Ming-Li to escape from Shanghai. And how did the watcher know to follow them? Who leaked the information about this operation? And why did they leak the information? Pilar wanted answers. She demanded answers. She could not wait to listen to Admiral Mahone's excuses or were there lies told to her so she would accept this easy assignment ? There was nothing easy about this operation. All the while there was friction at every turn. Her eyes were fixed on the submarine. She wanted to know why the sub did not pick them up at the rendezvous point as Admiral Mahone said they would be extracted from. Pilar knew someone wanted this assignment to fail. Her heart rate increased as she began to fit the pieces together. Who leaked the information, but who? Someone had to leak the information about this assignment. At this moment, she could not trust Admiral Mahone. Maybe the admiral wanted Pilar out of the way? Or was it Dusty, who planned to have her captured? Pilar had fire in her eyes glaring at the submarine as she stood frozen on the deck of the Ingersoll. At this moment, she was pleased Ming-Li was safely aboard the sub along with her mother, Connie and Henry were being taken care of by Doctor Khan, the sub's doctor. She hoped the glass from the blown-out windows did not penetrate into Chester's eyes. Pilar was thankful the watcher's bullet only grazed Nick's chest cavity. She pulled out of her pants pocket a water-soaked paper document. It was Candace's visa. She heard Ed yell from the side of the Ingersoll it was time to leave. Pilar climbed down the rope ladder onto the zodiac. She told Ed to motor to the bow where they would pick up the hanging line and take it to the submarine where the sub would tow the Ingersoll farther out to sea away from prying eyes of the Chinese navy. Pilar looked back at the Chinese destroyer sitting dead in the water knowing they got a licking too from Ingersoll's shells. As the zodiac approached the submarine, Pilar saw the skipper of the sub watching. Pilar asked for permission to come aboard and of course the skipper acknowledged her request.

"Welcome aboard the USS North Carolina." The skipper introduced himself with a half-smile. "I'm Commander Dave Griggs. We will get you home."

As Pilar stepped aboard the sub she asked, "Has everyone been taken care of below?"

"Yes. Our doctor is attending the needs of everyone." Commander Griggs turned away from Pilar and looked at Ed. "Hi Ed. You can secure the line to the stern of the sub. We'll tow the Ingersoll out to see to a depth were the Chinese will not be able to raise her." A sailor popped his head from the open hatch and motioned to Pilar. Pilar disappeared into the sub. He knew Ed from a previous mission. "Good job on tying the knot, sailor." He grinned at Ed. "As you know Ed, we can't take the zodiac aboard. You can fire your weapon into the pontoons so it will sink, all right?" The skipper watched Ed pull his forty-five pistol from his holster and fire several rounds into each of the pontoons of the zodiac. The skipper looked up at his executive officer, Lieutenant Commander Kirk Stapler standing inside the island. "All ahead slow and make sure the Ingersoll does not run over us." The order was given as the USS North Carolina slowly moved ahead pulling the slowly sinking Ingersoll.

The skipper followed Ed down into the sub and closed the topside hatch.

Commander Griggs asked Pilar to follow him to his conference compartment where he could talk confidently to Pilar. "Have a seat, Pilar."

"Thank you skipper." Pilar remarked looking into his soft brown eyes. "Could I have a glass of water? My throat is quite dry." She watched Commander Griggs snap his fingers.

A sailor poked his head in. "John, can you get Commander," He looked at Pilar. "I don't know your last name."

"Marshall. It's Marshall."

"Are you Captain Marshall's wife?"

"Yes sir, I am."

Commander Griggs turned his head and asked John, "Can you get a cold glass of water with ice for Lieutenant Commander Marshall, please? Or would you want a cup of coffee?"

"Water would be fine, skipper."

He watched as John disappear. "Pilar, I know you must be tired, but can you briefly summarize what happened?"

"Yes, sir. I work for Admiral Janis Mahone as her Intelligence Officer and I was asked if I would volunteer to escort Ming-Li out of Shanghai. Inside the city someone followed us. We don't know who, but he almost captured us as we prepared to leave the dock and head out to our rendezvous point off the coast of Shanghai. I was told a submarine was to pick us up. The Chinese coastal patrol almost caught us. Fortunately, there was a fog bank off the coast which we motored into to hide. So, we left the wooden boat and shoved it away from us swimming in the ocean knowing the patrol boat would follow our wooden boat in the fog. Hoping the sub would shortly rescue us. Suddenly, a zodiac appeared. I thought it was from a submarine, but my husband got the call from Sasebo to pick us up."

"I see." The skipper turned to see John appear with several glasses of water for Pilar along with several cookies and a cup of coffee for his skipper. "Thank you, John."

"Yes. Thank you, John." Pilar picked up one of the glasses of water and drank it all down. She looked at the skipper. "I'll never do this again. Someone leaked our presence in Shanghai. Somebody was following us. Thanks for picking us up, Commander." Pilar took hold of the second glass of water and slowly sipped it.

She did not touch the cookies.

"Pilar, you must have been under some strain in this assignment?"

"The point was to get Ming-Li out of Shanghai. I thought this assignment would be a simple one, but Nick and I needed to get away from the friction from this person who was watching us. We did not know who he was."

Lieutenant Commander Stapler appeared. "Skipper, we are off the Chinese continental shelf and the floor is at a depth of five thousand feet where we can sink the Ingersoll."

"Thank you, XO. You can untie the aft line. I know we have one of our Tomcats who will fire a missile at the Ingersoll and sink her in about a half an hour from now."

"Aye, aye, sir." The executive officer asked, "Shall we set a course back to Hawaii at our usual depth?"

"No." The skipper paused. "Set a course to Japan. Which will take about five to six hours to get there. All right, XO?" He looked at Pilar. "It is only about five- hundred miles to our naval base in Yokosuka, Japan."

"Perfect." The XO departed and headed to the operations center of the sub.

Pilar asked, "Is everyone taken care of, sir?"

"Of course." The skipper took a sip of his coffee.

"Oh, here is Candace's visa. Could you maybe try to dry it out?"

Commander Griggs reached for the wet visa. I'll get John to dry it out."

"Could you take me to my husband. I would like to know he is all right?"

Commander Griggs stood up holding his coffee mug. "Follow me, Pilar."

Pilar saw Chester laying in the bunk of the XO's compartment. Softly she asked, "Hi sailor, you doing all right?" She saw Chester open his eyes. She could see one of his eyes was quite red. Her eyes began to swell up with tears.

"Hi honey. Is everyone aboard?"

"Yes, everyone is aboard. We are all safe." Pilar took hold of his hand and held it tightly. "Thanks for coming to rescue us."

"You know, I'll always rescue you." He gave a small grin.

"How did you come to rescue us?"

"We got a call from Admiral Mahone to pick you up. We got lucky with Connie's destroyer moving at flank speed."

"Just in time, too."

"The doctor gave me a shot to relax. I'm feeling a little bit sleepy."

"I have been missing your morning salute in the shower. At least I have a place to hang my washcloth." Pilar saw a small grin on Chester's face. "You just close your eyes and I'll see you in a bit, all right?" Pilar leaned over and kissed him on his tender lips. A tear rolled down her cheek as she watched his eyes close and go to sleep. She looked around the XO's room to find a tissue to wipe the water flowing from her eyes. She did not find one but used her shirt sleeve. Pilar got up and went to see Nick. She found him in another compartment resting comfortably with Candace sitting by his side. "Hi Candace. How are you doing?"

Candace looked up to see Pilar enter the compartment. "He is resting quietly. The doctor gave him a shot to make him sleep."

"Good to know. But how are you doing?"

"I'm all right. This is a lot to take in. I can't believe I am on an American submarine. Everyone is so nice."

"Do you need anything to drink or some food?" asked Pilar as she touched Candace on her shoulder.

Candace turned away from looking at Nick. "We had some food earlier but I'm all right for now. Thanks for asking. Oh, I am wondering, where are we going?"

"To our naval base at Yokosuka, Japan."

"I have never been there."

"I'll check back with you in a bit. I'm going to check on everyone else. If you need anything, please let me know."

"Oh, did you see Margaret? She was talking to some cute sailors." Candace grinned.

"Good for her."

"I'll see you later." Candace watched Pilar leave the compartment.

Pilar asked a sailor where could she see the skipper. He pointed straight ahead and down the ladder. She found the skipper standing over the chart table and saw him pick up the microphone. Pilar heard over the ship's loudspeaker Commander Griggs' voice.

"Good morning everyone, this is the skipper. We have some guests aboard. So please give them our best navy courtesy. That is all."

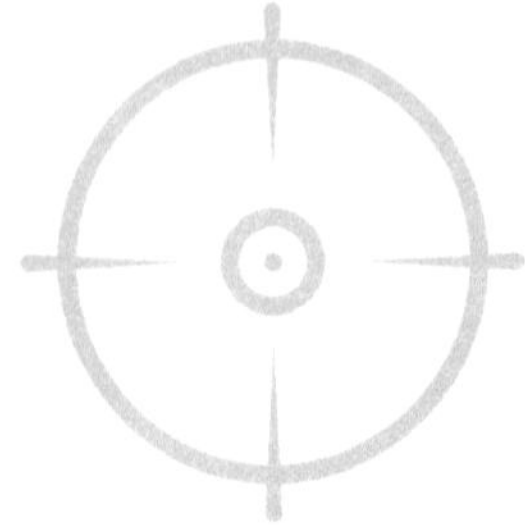

CHAPTER TWENTY- FIVE

After reviewing the satellite screen for twenty minutes and seeing the USS Ingersoll dead in the water, Dusty could not believe there was a small skirmish with a Chinese destroyer. He saw the Chinese destroyer stationary in the water several hundred yards away from the Ingersoll. He was pleased the Ingersoll could dish out what the Chinese started. He was relieved the submarine appeared to rescue everyone from the Ingersoll to the sub. He had to notify Admiral Mahone.

"Morning Admiral. This is Dusty Sommers."

"Morning, Dusty. Do have some news for me?"

"Yes, I do Admiral. Our satellite passed over the Ingersoll and we saw a Chinese destroyer stationary about two hundred yards away from the Ingersoll. There must have been a small battle between the Chinese destroyer and our destroyer. We could see the front deck section of the Ingersoll damaged and it appeared she was taking on water. We looked at the Chinese destroyer. We could see their destroyer was damaged, too. Then our sub appeared next to the Ingersoll taking on the sailors from our destroyer. Then the satellite moved away."

"Good to know, Dusty." Remarked Admiral Mahone.

"Admiral, would they be headed for Japan?"

"I would suspect they would. Probably, to our naval base at Yokosuka, Japan."

"When they arrive at your naval base, I'll requisition a private bus for them and move them quietly to a jet and transport them to Travis Air Force Base in California. I'm going to fly to Travis to meet them. We'll need to get our guest to Washington as soon as possible and be debriefed."

"Sounds like you are on top of the situation. Good to talk to you, Dusty." As Janis placed the phone on its cradle, she thought to herself that she might need to see Pilar when she arrives at Travis Air Force Base. Janis was tense for the past twelve hours hoping Pilar accomplished her assignment. Janis was sure Pilar might have some questions for her about the submarine not arriving at the proposed rendezvous. Knowing Pilar, she would be highly curious wanting to know why the sub did not meet them off the coast of Shanghai. Janis knew her Intelligence Officer wanted the right answers. Janis did not want Pilar to quit the navy.

***

The USS North Carolina was moored next to a tender at the Yokosuka naval base harbor in the late afternoon. The skipper communicated ahead when they entered the harbor to have an ambulance ready to take three sailors to the naval hospital. It took twenty minutes for the tugboat to gently push the sub next to the sub tender and tie the lines to secure the sub and set the ladder from the tender to the sub. There was a private bus waiting on the pier for Pilar, Ming-Li, her mother, Nick, Candace and Margaret. A Japanese gentleman in a dark suit exited the small bus and motioned to Pilar to gather her company into the bus. Pilar said goodbye to her husband,

Chester, Commander Resnis and Henry since the three of them needed medical attention. The driver commented that they were to be taken to the naval air base and board a jet. As they all sat inside the bus ready to move ahead, suddenly two shore patrol pickup trucks came roaring down the pier with their lights flashing. Behind the two shore patrol trucks, a black Chevy followed close by. One of the shore patrol trucks pulled in front of the bus to prevent the bus from departing the pier.

Pilar wondered what was going on. She exited the bus and was approached by the skipper of the submarine who was standing on the pier. She could not believe what he told her. The skipper said one of his sailors was brutally murdered. He explained to Pilar this had never happened in his command. Every sailor was hand selected and there was no anger among any of his sailors. All of his crew are professional sailors. He could not believe one of his sailors was killed.

The skipper of the USS North Carolina turned away from talking to Pilar and saw the Naval Investigative Service (NIS) agent exit his Chevy. The agent in charge of the investigation introduced himself to Commander Griggs. The agent turned to present himself to Pilar.

Agent Henderson was a serious man. His function was to investigate any criminal action involving the Navy or the Marine Corp. He was a heavy set, clean- shaven and he was a short black-haired man who smoked cigarettes. He listened to Commander Griggs explain they picked up Lieutenant Commander Pilar Marshall from the USS Ingersoll and they were on their way to be air lifted to United States with a guest from China. Agent Henderson pulled one of his cigarettes from inside his suit jacket and shoved his other hand into his pants pocket to collect a book of matches. He struck the match to light up his cigarette. The large smoke plume from the cigarette engulfed Commander Griggs' and Pilar's face. They both turned their heads to escape the large pocket of smoke. Pilar noticed a black button missing from the sleeve of the agent's suit jacket. The agent did not apologize for his rudeness. As Pilar looked down and away, she saw his loafers were not polished. The agent listened to Commander Griggs say the returning people who are on the bus remained in the mess area of the sub and they were no way near the sailor who was killed. Agent Henderson nodded his head and motioned to the shore patrol for the bus to depart.

As the bus headed on the road to the naval airport, Pilar sat alone on the bus wondering why the sailor was killed. From all the sailors aboard the North Carolina, they all seemed cordial. She could not detect any anger among any of the sailors she met. In fifteen minutes, the bus arrived at the air terminal. They all unloaded from the bus and they were escorted to a navy gulf wing jet. The captain of the jet said they would be flying to Adak, Alaska for refueling and then on to Travis Air Force Base in California. The travel time to Adak would be around six hours. The door to the jet closed. The jet engines increased their whine as they picked up more power to advance to the runway. Pilar fastened her seatbelt. She felt the brakes of the jet release as the jet engines increased more power to speed down the runway. The jet rotated upwards to the sky. She looked through the jet window watching the ground slowly fall below. The jet was airborne. Pilar could now let go and unwind. Pilar was mentally tired as she gazed looking down at the Japanese coastline. She wanted this assignment to be over. Asking herself, why did Nick's girlfriend, Candace and her friend, Margaret, tag along when Nick could have told Candace to stay behind? Then the two girls could have stayed behind on the shoreline, but they joined us in the boat. To Pilar, this did not make any sense. Why come along for a simple boat ride when Ming-Li, her mother and Nick would have to escape to the sub then the two girls would have to motor the boat back to shore? If it wasn't for the fog bank to hide them, the Chinese patrol boat would have captured all of them. Furthermore, Pilar questioned how did the watcher meet up with them at the pier holding a gun? If he was to assassinate Ming-Li, why didn't he shoot her, or maybe he was to escort her back to her office building? She closed her eyes and laid her head back. She wanted to be with her husband since she was concerned about the redness in one of his eyes, but she had to see this mission through and deliver Ming-Li to Dusty. Her eye lids felt heavy, she could not keep them open any longer, she fell sound asleep.

CHAPTER TWENTY-SIX

The navy gulf wing jet landed at Travis Air Force Base in the late afternoon. As everyone departed the jet, Dusty greeted every person. He was dressed in a dark suit and yellow tie as they stepped on the tarmac. He greeted Ming-Li with a warm smile and a welcoming hand-shake. They all boarded a small black van with dark tinted windows and headed toward an isolated office building ten minutes away on the base where Dusty could talk to everyone. Inside the building annex he placed Ming-Li and her mother in a separate room. The room had some snacks and sodas for them to eat. He explained they would be waiting until their jet to Washington was ready for takeoff. Dusty turned on the television for Ming-Li to watch while he talked to the others in another room. Also inside the room was an Air Force Policeman who was armed. He was to protect Ming-Li. The rest of the group was escorted to another room across the hall.

Dusty moved Nick and his girlfriend, Candace and Margaret to a large room.

There was snacks and cold sodas for them to enjoy. Dusty turned on the television for them to watch. Dusty asked Pilar to go into the adjacent room.

As Pilar sat down she launched into her questions aimed at Dusty. "Where was the sub that was to pick us up? It never showed up!"

Dusty closed the door and focused on Pilar. "You'll have to ask Admiral Mahone that question. She can best answer you." He heard the door to the room open.

Admiral Mahone dressed in her pressed khaki uniform cruised into the waiting room. She greeted Dusty and Pilar. She sat down next to Pilar. She could see anger on Pilar's face. She saw the serious weight of Pilar's eagle eyes as she focused on her. Admiral Mahone saw her Intelligence Officer without any makeup, no lipstick on her lips and her black hair was not combed and she could see her hair needed washing. She witnessed Pilar's Khaki shirt without her gold oak leaves on her collars and her slacks were terribly wrinkled.

Pilar offered a polite grin as she viewed the three silver stars on the admiral's collar. Her grin disappeared. In a deep voice Pilar uttered a formal greeting, "Afternoon Admiral Mahone."

"Good to see you, Pilar." The admiral's smile was always radiant. "I believe you have some questions for me?"

In a strong voice Pilar asked, "You told me a submarine was to pick us up. Well?" She paused gaining strength in her voice with her eyes locked on the admiral's smooth tanned face. "The submarine never showed up. We were sitting ducks hiding from the Chinese patrol boat. Fortunately, there was a fog bank which we could hide in waiting for the sub to pick us up." She paused again collecting her jaded anger. "So, where was the submarine?" Pilar looked away as she banged her tight fist on the table. Pilar was not in her cool and calm self, but out of character. She was fuming mad. She wanted an answer.

Admiral Mahone saw sharp steel daggers from Pilar's eyes. Before the admiral could answer Pilar, she was interrupted.

Pilar turned to face the admiral and launch another question, "We were waiting in the ocean after we sent the boat off in another direction away from us so the Chinese patrol boat would follow it, as we waited for the sub to pick us up. I want to know where was the sub? We could have been captured. Do you get my drift, Admiral Mahone?"

Admiral Mahone could see Pilar was about to come unglued. She could see the rage in Pilar's face. The admiral began to speak, but once again was cut short.

"Why did you lie to us about the submarine?"

The admiral with her sharp hawk eyes concentrated on Pilar's angry face. "Are you done Lieutenant Commander Marshall? So, I can answer your question?"

Pilar gazed at Dusty and then at the admiral, "Did you want us to fail on this assignment, Admiral Mahone?"

Admiral Mahone began to calmly speak as she placed her hand on Pilar's shoulder to try and calm Pilar's temper. "Pilar, I know you are angry, so let me try to unfold this for you."

"Yeah, I'd like to hear your excuses." Pilar looked at Dusty who was sitting next to her and listening to their heated conversation.

"Pilar, I have no excuses. If you would just listen to me for a moment, I can explain what happened. All right?" She watched Pilar sit in a frozen position glaring at her. The admiral replied, "I gave the order to have a submarine rendezvous off the coast of Shanghai, China. The sub was on its way from Hawaii when Admiral Ambrose, who was the head of the Pacific subs, learned of the operation. He recalled the sub back to Hawaii."

Pilar in a faint voice with piercing eyes asked, "Why?"

"Admiral Ambrose was not acting as a sailor but as a power-hungry shark not liking women in his navy. I explained to Admiral Ambrose the necessity of the sub. He would not listen to reason. The CNO called me and I told him of the necessity of the sub for this mission. We needed to extract someone from Shanghai, China."

Pilar asked, "Then what happened?"

"The CNO told me to call Sasebo, Japan and get a frigate or a destroyer to travel at flank speed to rescue you. There was still time for a rescue at the rendezvous point. I found out later that Admiral Ambrose, who was a four-star admiral lost one of his stars and was demoted to another duty station for disobedience to the Chief of Naval Operations. Nonetheless, a submarine was dispatched a few hours later from Hawaii to the rendezvous point."

Pilar looked at Dusty. With a strong voice she asked, "Did you know about this?"

Dusty replied, "At the outset, Pilar, the submarine was set to pick you up. Admiral Mahone notified me the sub was returned to Hawaii. She called me back and stated a ship would rescue you instead of the sub. The operation should have gone smoothly but we had to get Ming-Li out of Shanghai quickly. There was no time to plan her escape. We had our other agents on other assignments. I decided to ask Admiral Mahone for help recruiting a person with someone with your high qualifications to blend in and not be noticed in Shanghai. You, Pilar, filled this quota which. Thank you, Pilar," Dusty paused and touched her shoulder. "Pilar, this assignment was supposed to be an easy extraction for Ming-Li; however, it turned out to be a marathon for you. I understand it wasn't easy for you. I would venture to say, Nick was the key to assist you on this assignment. If it wasn't for his keen thinking at the boat dock, things would have turned the wrong way." Dusty paused again looking directly at her face. "Pilar, thank you so much for your tenacity on this covert assignment. I thank you."

Pilar realized the sincerity Dusty offered her. Her anger slowly disappeared and she calmed down. "You're welcome, Dusty."

In an adjacent room, stood a tall Air Force Policeman watching over Nick, Candace and Margaret. The television was on and they were relaxing. Margaret rose up to talk to the handsome Air Policeman. Suddenly she pulled her left arm up over his chest and struck him hard in the front of his neck cracking his trachea. Before the Air Policeman could react to the blow, he was on his knees gasping for air. She hit him on the back of his neck. The Air Policeman was unconscious laying on the carpet. She grabbed his revolver from his holster and cocked the gun.

Before Nick, who was sitting with Candace ten feet away, could do anything, he watched Margaret aim the gun and shoot one round into Nick. Candace was in disbelief. She could not believe her eyes her best friend took down the Air Policeman and shot Nick.

"Margaret," Candace hesitated with her eyes wide-open watching this event unfold. "What are you doing?" Candace followed with her eyes as Nick fell to the carpet.

Margaret shouted at Candace, "I hate Americans. I despise all greedy Americans! And I hate you being his girlfriend. You couldn't find a Chinese guy to fall in love with? Don't you know he works for an intelligence agency? How dumb can you be?" She aimed the gun at her best friend and fired one round but missed. She corrected her aim and fired the gun again. The third round hit Candace in her thigh. The bullet tore into her flesh and pounded into her thigh bone. Margaret heard her friend scream out in pain. Margaret exited the room and in the hall twenty feet away she saw another Air Force Policeman standing guard at the exit door. She raised the gun and took aim firing a single round at him. The bullet hit the Air Policeman and he fell limp to the linoleum hall floor.

Dusty, Admiral Mahone and Pilar heard a high-pitched scream from the other room. The Air Force Policeman standing guard heard the scream, too. He watched Dusty get up from his chair and opened the door to the other room. He heard Nick moaning on the carpet as he saw Candace holding her thigh. He saw her blood-soaked hands.

The stocky Air Policeman saw two people down on the carpet and he pulled his weapon from his holster. The alert Air Policeman saw the other Air Police laying quietly on the carpet and quickly asked, "Where is the other girl who was in this room?" The Air Police grabbed his shoulder mic and radioed several ambulances and called for support to the annex.

Candace with tears rolling down her face pointed to the other door. "She went out into the hall. I think she's crazy."

Dusty grabbed a bunch of table napkins and placed them on Candace's bullet wound. He saw Admiral Mahone grab a handful of paper napkins and roll Nick on his back placing the napkins on his sucking chest wound.

Pilar put it together. "She is out to kill Ming-Li, who is in the other room!" Pilar saw the Air Force Policeman cautiously exit the room and walkout into the hall.

His revolver was in his hand. He saw the fallen Air Patrolman motionless laying on the floor. Dusty followed the Air Policeman. They heard the loud pop. The sound came from the room where Ming-Li and her mother sat.

Dusty brushed next to the Air Policeman and grabbed the doorknob. He turned to open the door. He heard the Air Policeman say step away from the door. These were the last words Dusty heard.

Margaret had one item on her mind. Her assignment was to assassinate Ming- Li. Margaret saw Ming-Li sitting at the table. She smiled at Ming-Li and looked at the Air Patrolman standing guard. She was holding the gun behind her. She walked to the center of the room and aimed the revolver and fired one round instantly killing the Air Force Policeman. She watched him drop to the carpet like a falling rock. Margaret turned around and aimed the gun at Ming-Li. She nervously pulled the trigger. The bullet missed Ming-Li. Margaret's attention moved as she heard the door open and she fired several rounds into the door to stop their entry. The door immediately closed.

The Air Policeman felt Dusty brush next to him and watched as Dusty grabbed the doorknob. Before the Air Policeman could pull Dusty away from the door, he told Dusty to step away from the door. These were the last words Dusty would hear.

Pilar and the Air Force Policeman watched as Dusty was hit twice in the chest. Dusty's legs folded as he dropped to the floor. Pilar rushed and kneeled down to comfort Dusty.

Dusty looked up at Pilar. "Get her to Washington." Dusty closed his eyes.

Margaret's escape plan was to get off the base as fast as possible. She had to find a telephone and contact the undercover secret agent living in the San Francisco area. As fate or luck would have it, the black van which picked them up from the jet was parked outside of the annex. She knew she could not leave the hall since the Air Police laid blocking the door. It would take too much time to pull dead weight away from the door. The only escape would be through the window. She opened the window. Once outside, she did not see the driver in the van. Looking inside the van Margaret saw the key in the ignition. She climbed into the driver's seat and started up the van. She escaped.

The Chinese secret assembly of their agents are much better than the German Gestapo or the SS agents during WWII.

The agency for intelligence and state security in China is called the Ministry of State Security (MSS). This secretive agency is accountable for counterintelligence, foreign intelligence and of course political security. The MSS is located in the Haidian District of Beijing. The MSS is most energetic in computer analysis and cyber espionage as well as dirty tricks. This agency has over one hundred thousand agents. The MSS acts like a blend of the Central Intelligence Agency, National Security Agency and the Federal Bureau of Investigation. The MSS is quite active in Canada, Mexico and Cuba. Margaret has been watching Nick for the past few months. Margaret's best friend, Candace, did not know she was employed by the MSS.

The Air Force Policeman with his revolver drawn cautiously opened the door and entered the room. Pilar was right behind him. She saw Ming-Li alive.

"Ming-Li, you all right?" Pilar asked. She saw her head nod yes.

The Air Policeman noticed the fallen Air Policeman laying on the carpet and saw the window was open. He looked outside as the van was speeding away. He turned to Pilar. "She must have taken the van. Don't worry, the base is locked down." The Air Policeman exited the room and walked down the hall stepping over Dusty. He saw a pool of blood laying underneath the dead Air Policeman. He grabbed hold of his arm and pulled him away from the door. He heard the sirens grow louder as the ambulance advanced to the annex. The two medics rushed into the annex. They saw the dead Air Policeman and saw another body. One medic placed his fingertips on Dusty's neck. The two medics carried him into the ambulance and quickly drove away. A second pair of medics entered the annex. The Air Policeman pointed for the medics to go into the other room. The medics placed Nick and Candace on two separate stretchers carrying them into the ambulance. A third set of medics arrived and picked up the three dead Air Force Policeman and drove silently away.

Pilar saw Admiral Mahone standing in the doorway looking down at Dusty as he was carted away. Pilar remarked in anger, "I can't believe this happened." Pilar looked up at Admiral Mahone. "How am I going to get Ming-Li and her mother to Washington? I'm too tired." Again, there was added friction to the assignment.

"All I want to do is take a shower and clean up." She followed the admiral to an empty room.

The Admiral thought for a moment and then spoke, "Pilar, how about this plan? I drove up from Moffett Naval Air base. My car is outside. The base is thirty-five miles south of San Francisco. We can drive back to the base and we can take the jet I flew in from Hawaii and take it to Washington. The drive time is only about an hour to the naval base. Sound good, Pilar?"

Pilar with a tired face looked at the admiral and nodded, yes. "Fine. I'll gather Ming-Li and her mother."

On the ride back to Moffett Naval Base, Pilar was tense because of the shooting. Sitting in the passenger side, she reached to turn on the radio and tried to relax. Pilar listened to the popular rock group called America over the radio.

She thought of her husband, Chester. She missed his strong lips which kissed her so gently. She hoped his eye would be all right. Pilar glanced at Admiral Mahone and said, "If I see that Margaret again, I will shoot her, dead. I'm surprised she got away. I hope the Air Police find her." She looked back at Ming-LI and her mother sitting in the back seat. They both were looking out at the cars passing by. They did not seem to be too shaken up by the shooting. "I hope Nick and his girlfriend, Candace and Dusty will be all right."

Admiral Mahone mentioned, "She was a trojan horse. A very cleaver trojan horse the Chinese security set in motion. I'm sure she was watching you and Nick. Somehow, she learned of Ming-Li's leaving China. She was just waiting for the right time. Fortunately, she failed in her mission. We'll be on the base shortly where we can get you, Ming-Li and her mother cleaned up with a new set of clothes." She looked over at Pilar. She saw her eyes closed with her head resting against the headrest. The admiral was relieved her Intelligence Officer accomplished her covert assignment. She feared Pilar might resign her commission in the navy. She did not want Pilar to quit the navy. Pilar had the strength and insight in her forward thinking on foreign affairs. The admiral took a deep breath noting she could have lost Pilar due to the pig- headed incompetent idiot who did not release the sub to Shanghai. Admiral Ambrose had no managerial integrity. It was only his bark where people were afraid of. She was pleased Admiral Taylor had the brilliance to fire Ambrose. Admiral Mahone looked into the rear-view mirror wanting to see Ming-Li. She saw her sitting quietly and peering out watching the cars driving by. The admiral wondered why Ming-Li escaped from China. It could not be for the freedom living in the United States? Ming-Li had all the freedom living in China. It was something bigger than her freedom.

Dusk turned to night. It was a clear warm evening in California. Margaret parked the van several miles away at a dark isolated section on the base perimeter. The van sat in between two twenty-foot-tall perimeter security lights. Off in the distance, Margaret could see the jets and hear the roar of the jet engines landing and taking off on the runway. There was freedom on the other side of the fence. The fence was ten feet tall with barbed wire on the top rail.

Also, there was a thick wire running on the bottom of the fence. She knew the van could not penetrate the fence. The fence had two-inch-thick aluminum columns ten feet apart holding the cyclone fence. She could not crawl underneath the fence. She had nothing to dig underneath the fence. She turned the lights off to the van. She sat inside the van, thinking. She knew the base police would be looking for her. She had not failed in her assignment, only postponed the killing of Ming-Li. Margaret was clever. Clever enough to get herself boxed in at Travis AFB. She was trapped. However, she was taught how to evade and escape. She had to think about her rapid escape.

She remembered her instructor at the academy told her about Carpe Diem, seize the day or seize the opportunity in front of you to escape. Margaret started up the van and pulled the van next to the fence line. She saw the tall standing light pole was three feet outside the fence. She backed the van right next to the cyclone fence. When she heard the side of the van scrape the fence, she knew she was close enough. She turned the engine off and climbed out of the driver's window to the roof of the van. Standing on top of the van, she quickly studied what she would have to do to escape. Riding all along the ten-foot fence line, there were three strands of barbed-wire at a forty-five-degree angle which she would have to jump up and hop over and reach to grab the light pole. She could grab hold of the five-inch aluminum column pole which supported the overhead security light rising twenty feet tall. She knew she could not jump over the barbed-wire and free-fall down to the ground outside the fence. It was too dangerous. A ten-foot fall to the ground would be easy, but she might land and twist her ankle or in the landing or she might break her wrist or arm. That possibly was too risky. The better plan was for her to jump up and over the barbed-wire where she could grab hold of the light pole, which was three, four or five feet away from the fence. She would then slide down the pole and she would be free.

Margaret realized she would have to act quickly since anyone from one hundred yards away could see her on top of the van as the security light illuminated the area. She did not have too much time to ponder the situation. She looked behind her. She saw there were no cars coming on the perimeter road.

She had to move. She did not want to fail. Failure meant disgrace. She placed one foot on the supporting arm holding the three strands of barbed-wire and balanced herself placing her other foot on top of the extending string of wire. Her arms gently moved back and forth balancing her body on top of the wire. All she had to do now was to spring toward the light pole. She was seconds away from freedom. Margaret's athletic legs were ready to move. She bent down and set to spring forward. Her eyes concentrated on the light pole. She looked down at the ground and back up to the aluminum pole. She jumped high and forward to the pole. Margaret extended her arms outward. She reached the pole and hugged it like a long-lost friend. Her chin banged into the aluminum pole and then her chest slammed against the pole. However, the top of her running shoe caught hold of one of the barbs. She moaned as her leg stretched behind her caught by the barbed-wire. She was now holding on the light pole as her right leg was hanging in mid-air swinging trying to grab hold of the pole while her other leg was stretched behind her preventing her escape. She tugged on her left leg to pull her foot free. She did not want to pull out of her shoe. She jerked her leg. She could feel the sharp needle like barb attacking her toes. She moaned. Margaret jerked her leg one more time. Her body came crashing forward toward the light pole. When she hit the light pole she wrapped one of her legs around it supporting herself. She slowly inched her way down to freedom. As she began to walk away she could feel pain from her toes. She glanced down and saw a red mark on the top of her torn running shoe. The barb must have cut into one of her toes. It was time to think as she walked along in the darkness outside the base. Her lips and her tongue required moisture. With all of the excitement, her body burned up a tremendous amount of water leaving her to notice her mouth was full of cotton. Her mouth felt like a dry desert. She needed water so she would not become dehydrated. Margaret felt no remorse as she walked along the side of the highway thinking about how she killed three American Air Force Policemen and shooting her friend, Candace and her American boyfriend. She had to get to a phone to call her contact for help. Her contact worked at a shoe repair shop on Polk Street in San Francisco. Her next move would be to get cleaned up and fly to Washington, D.C. She remembered Sommers said he was from the Alexander Hamilton Foundation in Washington. She bet this is where Ming-Li will be by tomorrow. She still had a chance to kill her. She had no purse and no money.

Now, she had to turn herself into a con-artist. She was sure some lonely air force guy would certainly pick up a cute Chinese girl walking alone on the highway.

CHAPTER TWENTY-SEVEN

At the naval air base, the admiral arranged for Pilar to freshen up and get into her naval khakis with her gold lieutenant commander oak leaves on her collars. Ming-Li and her mother were able to get cleaned up and into some fresh civilian clothes. After a good night's sleep at the base hotel and a solid breakfast the next morning, they would board the admiral's jet from Moffet Naval Air Base to Andrews AFB. Before their flight to Andrews, the admiral had time and telephoned Director Laube ahead informing him they would be bringing Ming-Li. She also called the hospital at Travis Air force base checking on Candace, Nick and Dusty. As the jet started down the runway, she told Pilar that Candace's gunshot wound would take time to heal naturally. The bullet only fractured the femur bone and she would be released in two days. Nick's chest wound was an in and out. He'll have some stiff chest muscles and he would be released in two days' time, too. The head nurse let the admiral know that Nick proposed to Candace and she said yes. The admiral asked about Dusty Sommers. The nurse said he was on the critical list. The bullet had nicked a pulmonary artery. He had lost four pints of blood and he was fortunate to be alive. The admiral will inform the director about the incident at Travis Air Force Base. Admiral Mahone knew Pilar needed to tell the Director Laube at the Foundation about the assignment. The flight to Andrews was uneventful. The admiral noticed Pilar was silent on the six-hour flight. At Andrews Air Force base, the admiral secured a loaner air force car for their short trip to the Alexander Hamilton Foundation. The drive time from the air force base to Vienna, Virginia was less than an hour.

The admiral located the unassuming three-story brick building in Vienna, Virginia. She pulled around to the back of the building and parked the car. The receptionist at the foundation corralled the admiral, Pilar, Ming-Li and her mother into the elevator. The director was dressed in his dark navy-blue three-piece suit as he offered a handshake to Admiral Mahone. "Good to see you, admiral."

The admiral smiled and extended her hand to greet the director. "Good to see you again." She turned to Pilar and said, "This is Lieutenant Commander Pilar Marshall. She undertook the assignment."

With a warm grandfatherly smile, the director said, "Well done, Commander. And thank you for your great endeavor on this covert assignment. I'm sure it wasn't easy." He watched Pilar slowly move her mouth to a half smile. He recognized Pilar wasn't too pleased.

When the director offered a genuine smile, Pilar noticed the yellow stained teeth probably from too much coffee the director was drinking and then answered, "No sir. It wasn't easy in Shanghai, China." She turned to introduce Ming-Li. "This is your guest, Ming-Li and her mother."

"I am so glad to meet you, Ming-Li and your mother." The director offered a handshake to both of them.

"We are happy to be in America. Thank you for having us. My mother does not speak too much English." Ming-Li offered a small grin to the director.

The director turned to the other gentleman in the room. "This is Nick Briscoe. He will be taking you upstairs for indoctrination. He will be taking over for Dusty." The director said softly, "Nick, please escort Ming-Li and her mother upstairs for processing into America." He looked at Ming-Li. "Upstairs you will receive a social security number and a Virginia driver's license and one credit card." He turned to Nick and commented, "Nick, please make sure Ming-Li has a bank account, too." He turned to Ming-Li. "Nick will get you both settled in with valid American requirements for your permanent stay. After which, you will be taken to one of our safe houses outside the city where you will be debriefed." He watched Ming- Li nod her head, yes.

Nick escorted Ming-Li and her mother to the elevator.

The director asked the admiral and Pilar if they would like something to drink. "Please, have a seat." He locked on to Pilar. "Pilar, I would like to know how the assignment went?" The director took his seat behind his desk.

Pilar grit her teeth as she focused on the deep cut lines on the old spymaster's granite stone face. When she took her seat, she saw the top of his desk was cluttered with folders and scattered papers. She began to explain the friction she ran into on the assignment. "I'll tell you what happened. I'll tell you what really happened." Pilar moved from a relaxed position sitting in her chair to the edge of her chair.

The director could tell from her raised voice she was angry. "I gather the assignment extracting Ming-Li from Shanghai was not an easy one. Right?"

Pilar replied, " At first the mission was easy, getting to the porcelain shop picking up Ming-Li. However, Nick and I recognized this guy was following us. This guy, who was wearing a baseball cap, kept watching us. On our way to collect a boat, I thought we lost him. He showed up at the dock." She paused to think. Pilar put it together. "Now, I remember Candace's friend, Margaret, who came along for the ride. She went into the fishing shack and she must have used the telephone to call someone. I'll bet she called the watcher. How else could he have known we were boarding the boat to get away? How else would Margaret come along for the ride to the rendezvous point? It all gets clear, as I think about it."

The director interrupted her. "Who is Candace and Margaret?"

Pilar leaned forward as she crossed her legs looking at the director. "Candace is Nick's girlfriend who was going to the market with her friend, Margaret. Candace wanted to come along to help us navigate through Shanghai, because Nick could have got us lost getting Ming-Li out of the city."

"I see. Please, continue, Pilar."

"At the dock, the watcher appeared. He had a gun and ordered us out of the boat. Fortunately, Nick used an oar to push the watcher back. He was off balance as he fell backwards hitting his head knocking him out in the wooden boat across from our boat. I jumped into the boat and pulled off his sunglasses and I did not recognize his face. I took the gun and then we motored away to get to the rendezvous point." Pilar watched as the director opened a folder on his desk.

"Pilar, could it be this gentleman?" The director handed the black and white five by seven picture to her. He waited for her response.

Pilar studied the black and white photo. "Yeah. That's the guy." Pilar looked up at the director. "Who is he?" Pilar handed the photo to Admiral Mahone.

The spymaster said, "His name is Elliot Farnsby. He works for the British intelligence. Dusty asked him to shadow you for support. The next day, I received a call from MI6 informing me Elliot Farnsby was a double agent. I notified Dusty. It appears Margaret was an undercover Chinese security agent. Would you know where is she now?"

"As we reached the rendezvous point, there was a small Chinese patrol boat coming toward us. As fate would have it, there was a fog bank offshore. We hid in the fog waiting for the submarine to pick us up." Pilar turned her head and looked at the admiral. "There was no submarine to pick us up. A zodiac picked us up from our destroyer. Our destroyer, the USS Ingersoll, was waiting for us to return in international waters. That is when a Chinese destroyer spotted us and fired on us in international waters. One of the Chinese's salvos hit the bridge of the Ingersoll ripping up the bridge of the Ingersoll.

Captain Marshall, who is my husband, the skipper of the destroyer, Commander Resnis and Henry the helmsman were injured. Suddenly, the sub appeared on our starboard side and we escaped. The Ingersoll fired a few shots at the Chinese destroyer and disabled it."

The director asked, "Where is your husband now?"

"The sub took us to Yokosuka Naval base in Japan. Chester, Connie and Henry are in the naval hospital." She watched as the director picked up his phone and talked to his executive secretary asking her to get a hold of the hospital in Yokosuka naval base and inquire on the status of Captain Marshall, Commander Resnis and the sailor named Henry. "Then we boarded a flight to Travis Air Force Base. That is when the fun really started."

"What?" Asked a puzzled director as he leaned forward listening. His arms rested on his desk. He listened intently.

Pilar continued, "At Travis Air Force Base, we were in separate rooms relaxing waiting for Dusty to debrief us. This is when Margaret was in a separate room across from our room and killed the first Air Policeman and took his gun. She then entered the room where Ming-Li was sitting. She shot the Air Policeman guarding the exit down the hall and killed the Air Force Policeman in the room where Ming- Li sat. She escaped through a window. We don't know where she went on the base."

"I see. Was this where Dusty was shot, too?"

"Yes. Margaret also shot her girlfriend, Candace and Nick."

The director's phone chirped. He picked up the receiver and listened for a moment. "Thank you. Amy." He set the phone on its cradle. " He looked up at Pilar. "Pilar, Amy is my executive secretary and my operation's manager here at the foundation. I plucked her away from working at a dentist office. I recognized she had the brilliance and intelligence as well as she is easy on the eyes for this job at the foundation. Once the FBI cleared her for the needed top-secret clearance, we hired her. Anyway, she got hold of the nurse at the hospital. Your husband, Captain Marshall was released and headed back to Hawaii. Commander Resnis was also released. She and the sailor, Henry, are both headed back to San Diego."

"Thank you, Director Laube." Pilar sat back into her chair relieved to know Chester was all right and Connie and Henry were on their way back to duty. She sat in a more relaxed position.

"Sure. Pilar, Mr. Briscoe will be back shortly. If you could describe what this Margaret looks like. I'm confident she escaped to the Chinese hide-away cell in San Francisco. The Chinese have a secret network in the United States." He turned to face the admiral. "On the strength of Pilar's comment, it is your turn Admiral Mahone. Why didn't one of your subs arrive at the rendezvous point as Dusty told me the sub would?"

"The order was given to have the USS Connecticut cruise to the rendezvous point off the coast of Shanghai, China. It was on its way when Admiral Ambrose learned that the Connecticut was on a surreptitious mission. He called me and recalled the sub. We were in a heated conversation. Unfortunately, he did not want a woman naval officer directing one of his submarines to the shores of China. I told him he just sealed the people waiting for the sub their fate. He did not care. The conversation ended. The CNO, who is Admiral Taylor, called me. He listened to my plea for help. He suggested that I call Sasebo Naval base and get a frigate or a destroyer to the rendezvous point. As luck would have it, Captain Chester Marshall received my call and grabbed the destroyer USS Ingersoll. We were lucky to have Commander Resnis and her highly skilled skeleton crew travel at flank speed to the rendezvous point. Once at the point but waiting in international waters, a zodiac was dispensed to retrieve everyone at the rendezvous point. This is where a Chinese destroyer appeared and fired on our destroyer. The Ingersoll was damaged, but the Ingersoll returned fire and disabled the Chinese destroyer. The Chinese destroyer was dead in international waters. The USS North Carolina was dispatched from Hawaii and arrived next to the Ingersoll and retrieved everyone. The sub towed the sinking Ingersoll out to sea where it was sunk to the depths of the Davy Jones' Locker. So, the incident never happened. The sub cruised to Yokosuka Naval base in Japan."

The director looked at Pilar and Admiral Mahone. "Thank you, both for your comments. This brings me up to speed on this mission." He leaned forward in his chair and tapped with his fingertips on his desk. "What concerns me now, is that we have a loose cannon on the horizon. Her name is Margaret, who must work for the Chinese intelligence service. I am sure as the day is long, she has an open road to Washington." The director paused and looked away, thinking. He returned his eyes to the admiral and Pilar. Abruptly, his telephone chirped. Director Laube answered the call. He listened and set the phone back on its cradle. "That was Nick Briscoe on the phone. Ming-Li has requested that both of you accompany her to our safe house. I am sure that this Margaret will attempt to continue her mission. She has probably changed to a blonde wig and a business suit to evade anyone looking for a black-haired Chinese girl in standard blue jeans wearing a polo shirt. Since you two know what she looks like, it would be advisable for you both to come along in case Margaret shows up. Besides, I'm sure Ming-Li will be comforted by seeing you both. A van is waiting for us. Shall we go? " He watched Admiral Mahone and Pilar rise and walk to the elevator.

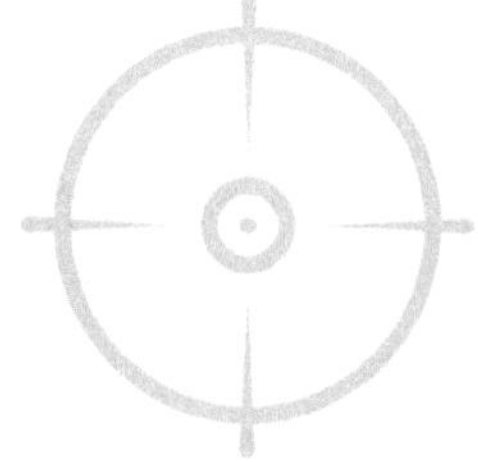

CHAPTER TWENTY-EIGHT

While they were sitting comfortably and watching the cars travel on the highway in the black air-conditioner van, the director explained where he was taking them. "The Manassas Country Club which has a Golf Course and Hotel suites are located south of Vienna, Virginia. Our ride will take about thirty minutes. The other intelligent agencies have their country estates and farmhouses for their guests, but we have our own secure private golf course and hotel for our guests." The director turned to Ming-Li, "Ming-Li, you and your mother will be staying in one of our guest suites for a couple of weeks until we get you a place to live in Vienna. You'll be working for us." He offered her a warm continuing smile. "Oh Ming-Li, we have around the clock security on the grounds at the country club. Have you ever played golf?"

"No, I have not played golf. It looks easy."

The black van stopped at the entrance to the country club. A marine guard recognized Director Laube and viewed the other occupants in the van. With a hand wave, he motioned the driver to proceed.

The director continued, "The game requires patience and it is quite relaxing and at various times highly frustrating, especially, if you lose a golf ball in the rough or in the water hazard." He looked at Amy. "Do you hear the approaching thunder? It will be raining very soon. Please escort Ming-Li and her mother to the numbered suite and get them settled in. Oh, see Gail, who is the hotel administrator, to get their suite number." The director watched Amy escort Ming-Li and her mother across the parking lot to one of the suites. The director looked outside. The late summer evening quickly turned darker with threatening heavy rain clouds. "Oh my, there goes another clap of thunder." He turned to Admiral Mahone and Pilar and said, "Since it will be pouring rain in about 15 minutes, why don't you stay for dinner until the rain clears off and then we can take you back to the Foundation to pick up your car?" He watched them both agree with a half-smile. "Good. You'll meet Hamilton. He is our chef. He can cook you anything you wish." He pointed the way to the cozy dining room.

***

Margaret hitched a ride to San Francisco. Some airman from Travis AFB gave her a lift and delivered her to Polk Street. She gave him a song and a dance about how her date ditched her. The airman bought her story completely. She also weaseled ten bucks from him and then gave him a kiss. She was good at her craft. She was dropped off near the shoe store. Margaret waved bye to the airman as he drove off. She walked to the shoe repair store. Once at the store she gave the counter-sign which got her upstairs to her controller, Mr. Lucky Tong. Mr. Tong liked his American name, Lucky. He enjoyed working undercover in America. He was offered another position in Atlanta, Georgia, but turned it down. He enjoyed the fresh ocean air in San Francisco. He was a heavy-set Chinese man. Lucky sent a coded email message to Beijing ordering more leather soles for his shoes which was coded to identified Margaret, so she could continue her mission to assassinate Ming-Li. His email was returned promptly acknowledging

Margaret as one of their covert dragons. After reading her file, Mr. Tong was concerned Margaret did not have a boyfriend, but liked the girls. The dragon masters have molded Margaret into a solid predator. Lucky knew she would be resourceful in her pursuit killing the traitor, Ming-Li.

The next morning, Mr. Tong purchased an airline ticket to Washington, D.C. for her and he gave her a map of Washington and of the surrounding area. While at the safe house Margaret unfolded the map, her eyes located Vienna, Virginia. She recalled Farnsby telling her there is a private golf course south of Vienna and this is the Foundation's safe location for their new guests. Margaret selected a set of new business clothes and a blonde wig, Margaret cleaned up rather well. She received a credit card and two thousand American dollars for her trip. She exited the shop by the back door and stepped down to the dirty alley where a taxi was waiting. She crossed the path of a black cat who was in the alley looking for food. At the San Francisco Airport she bought a pair of sunglasses which covered up her Pacific Asian eyes. She did not want any American guys looking at her cute face.

Her flight landed in Washington, D.C. around two in the afternoon. Margaret rented a car with no problem showing her California Driver's License and insurance papers. Mr. Tong was a master at forged documents. In fact, he gave himself a Ph. D. in engineering from Stanford University after he hacked into the university's computer system and entered his name receiving a doctorate. He was proud of his accomplishment. He had his diploma framed and hung his diploma on the wall of his shop behind his cash register, so his shoe customers could recognize his brilliance. They called him Doctor Tong. He was well known in his community by donating funds to the local elementary school for the little children. Before Margaret left on her mission, he mentioned to her that if she was successful, she would be promoted to division manager in London, England. She would direct other dragons on secret missions. The clandestine London office was the prize every dragon wanted. Working in London meant prestige, honor, but most of all, it meant earning more money.

Admiral Mahone asked, "Is there a menu we could look at?" She turned to look at Director Laube. "I like these light blue linen tablecloths." She glanced at Pilar.

"No. There is no menu. The waiter will come by and you can tell him or her what you might like for dinner. By the way, our chef makes the best cheesecake with fresh sliced strawberries on the side and it is to die for." He looked away from the admiral as the waiter approached their table. "Pilar, why don't you order first?" The director looked outside as he heard another clap of thunder. "Wow, look at it rain outside." He could see sheets of rain pour down on the green golf course.

Pilar looked up to the waiter. "I'll have a rib-eye steak, medium well, baked potato with a salad."

The waiter asked, "What would you like on your salad?"

"Oh, vinegar and oil, please."

"And something to drink?"

"Iced tea would be fine, thank you." Pilar sat back in her soft chair and looked outside watching the rain pour down in buckets.

The waiter looked at Admiral Mahone. "And for you, Admiral?" "I'll have the same, please."

"Medium well?"

"Yes."

"And for you, Director."

"Let's keep this simple."

I'll have the same. Please bring us three glasses of your house merlot wine." He watched as Admiral Mahone excuse herself. He glanced at Pilar. He gently placed his hand on her shoulder. "Pilar, I want to personally say, thank you, for your commitment in getting Ming-Li through this mission. I can tell this mission was not in your pay grade, but you had the strength in solving various tight situations in Shanghai. I cannot over emphasis how America is indebted to you for your service. I know there should have been more time for this assignment, but it was the only time Ming-Li could get away." The director looked directly into the smooth tan completion of Pilar. "Pilar, you thought with forethought on how to get away from the watcher, Farnsby. Little did you know Margaret was a Chinese undercover spy. Even Nick did not know. You had the courage to continue with your assignment. You did not quit. Your move to send the boat away and get your team into the water was truly brilliant." He watched as Pilar nod her head, yes. Then he saw Pilar slowly turn her head away from him to look at the pouring rain. He recognized she was under a great strain during this mission. He viewed a few tears running down her face. "Pilar," the director commented, "Those tears running from your eyes are stress tears which are telling your mind you are healing from this ordeal. You'll be fine once you get back to Hawaii and be with Chester. He is your rock." He saw Pilar wipe the few tears from her face.

Margaret drove in the pouring rain to the Manassas Country Club. At the main gate, the Marine could hardly hear the occupant in the car as the rain came down in buckets pounding on the car roof. He heard she was a new employee. Margaret showed the marine her California's driver's license. The marine directed her to park in the visitors parking section which was fifty yards away. She parked the car and turned off the engine. Since it was close to six o'clock, Margaret thought for a moment. They would be eating dinner. She opened the car door and quickly ran into the administration building. She asked where the dining room was located?

The marine guard on administrative duty pointed across the parking lot. There was no one else in the room. She moved next to the marine taking off her sunglasses. She saw the marine gaze at her attractive Pacific Asian complexion. "When do you get off duty?" She asked him. She heard him comment in two hours. She needed a weapon. This was her chance to collect his gun. She asked if he could rub her neck for a moment and get the muscles working again? He agreed. She felt his strong fingers ease her tired muscles. After a few minutes of a tender neck and shoulder massage, Margaret quickly turned around and forced a smile. She struck him hard in the marine's trachea. She watched him drop like a rock to the carpet. She pulled his revolver from his holster and smashed his head with the butt of the gun. She pushed him underneath the administration desk so no one could see him. Margaret was in the river of hate. She hated Americans.

She checked the gun to see if it was loaded with bullets. She placed the revolver inside her purse. It was pouring rain outside. She would have to run across the parking lot to the dining room which was twenty-five yards away. She saw a black van parked in front of the dining hall. She thought they must be there. Margaret grabbed a folded newspaper from the trash container placing it over her head as she exited the administration building.

Director Laube asked, "So, how did Dusty get shot?"

Pilar answered, "The Marine told him not to stand in front of the door since Margaret was in the other room. He told Dusty to step away. By then, Dusty was turning the door handle to the room and two shots came through the door hitting Dusty."

"I see." The director tapped his fingers on the table. "A fatal mistake on his part. He should have been more aware of the situation."

"Do you think Margaret will show up here?"

"Naugh." The director looked at the waitress advancing toward their table with three large goblets of red wine. "Here she comes." He watched as Pilar looked toward the waitress. "Pilar, this merlot wine is one of Virginia's best wines. Full of body, with notes of cherry and mildly sweet. I hope you enjoy the taste." He observed as the waitress set the glasses of wine in front of them.

"Welcome back, Admiral." He watched Admiral Mahone take her seat. He took hold of his wine glass and raised it. "A toast to you both and may your years be long and healthy. Oh, and may all of your battles be won at sea."

The waitress asked, "Table for one?" She watched as Margaret stomp the rain from her wet slacks and soaking shoes. "At least you had a newspaper to cover your hair." The waitress smiled at her and took hold of the wet newspaper and threw it into the trash.

"Oh, I can sit at the bar."

"Follow me."

Seated at the bar Margaret ordered a glass of white wine. She placed her heavy purse on the chair next to her. She thanked the bartender as she slowly turned her head and looked across the room behind her. She spotted Pilar sitting at the dining table about twenty-five feet away, but she wondered who was the older man sitting at the table? She recognized the admiral sitting at the table.

Margaret did not see Ming-Li. The bartender returned with a chilled glass of white house wine. Margaret took a sip from her glass. She was thinking where was Ming-Li? She heard someone enter the dining room. Looking down at her purse, she glanced at the entry hall to see who was there. Her eyes caught hold of a young administrative person standing alone. She watch the girl walk over to the table where Pilar was sitting. Margaret saw the girl lean over and talk to the older gentleman. Margaret turned around to address her wine.

Amy leaned over and spoke into the director's ear. "Director."

The director saw Amy was visibly shaken. "What's wrong, Amy?"

"Ah, I was at the admin building and I did not see the marine on duty, so I walked behind the desk." She took hold of the director's shoulder. She felt ill.

"What's wrong?"

"Ah, the marine was shoved underneath the desk. I thought he was getting something, but I think he is dead. I don't feel so good."

"Here. Take a seat. I want you to sit down." The director saw fear in Amy's face. The director snapped his fingers. He saw the waitress appear at the table. "Please get Amy a shot of cognac."

Pilar noticed from Amy's face something was wrong. "What is it director?"

The director looked at Admiral Mahone and Pilar. "I don't want to alarm you but the marine on duty in the admin building is dead." The director took hold of Amy's shoulder and gave it a gentle but firm pulse. He watched as the waitress arrived with the cognac. "Here, take a sip of this. It will steady your nerves." He watched as she took a sip of the cognac. "Amy, where is Ming-Li?"

"She and her mother will be coming to dinner shortly. I'm going to get up and get a cold soda at the bar. I'll be right back."

Director Laube saw the blonde woman sitting alone at the bar. From his years of covert missions, the director put it together. The person at the bar must be our predator. How she got here, he did not know. There must be a leak somewhere. We have to get help. He sat thinking. His mind was moving like a fast freight train from his years of tight situations on various missions in the O.S.S.. He watched Amy walk to the bar and ask the bartender for a cold soda. As Amy turned holding the can of soda in her hand, the predator was off her stool and grabbed Amy.

Holding her tight against her body, Margaret raised the 45-caliber handgun and aimed it at Amy's ribs.

Margaret looking coldly at Pilar and said in a strong demanding voice, "Where is Ming-Li?"

Director Laube was in this type of dangerous situation during WW II. Where a Gestapo agent held one of his close friends with a Lugar pistol. The director knew how to handle the situation. As he stood up from the dining room table, he turned toward Pilar. He quickly pulled from his waist his black twenty-two framed polymer Taurus which held ten rounds. He handed the gun to Pilar. His suit coat jacket covered his move, so the predator could not see him handing the pistol to Pilar. Standing and looking down at Pilar, he softly said, "You have to cock it. The safety is off." He then turned to face the predator.

Suddenly, Ming-Li quietly appeared in the dining room. Margaret noticed her standing ready to enter the room. "There you are. You traitor!" She coldly aimed the gun at her.

Something had to happen. It wasn't a checkmate just yet, only a check. The director knew Pilar could not shoot Margaret with Amy in front of her. Amy realized it was up to her to make a move on the chess board. Amy could not pull away from her attacker, because Margaret held her too tight around her waist, so she remembered from her self-defense class what to do in this situation. Amy placed her weight on her right leg while lifting her left leg high enough to jam her foot back toward Margaret's left foot. If her move did not work, Amy knew she would be shot. Amy was determined to get it right the first time. With a powerful downward push, Amy jabbed with a rapid stomp of her shoe to the inside ankle of Margaret. Amy then grabbed hold of Margaret's hand which was holding her at her waist. She selected a finger and pulled the finger back as hard as she could, which released her from Margaret's hold. Amy rolled forward on the carpet and away from Margaret.

After receiving the ankle blow from Amy, Margaret bellowed out a loud cry. Her reflex was to pull her finger on the trigger. A loud pop exploded from the gun. The shot went wild hitting the painting on the dining room wall.

"Now, Pilar. Aim and shoot! " barked the director.

Pilar took aim. She pulled the trigger. The bullet missed Margaret. Pilar fired again. She missed. Anger filled her mind. Pilar fired a third time. The shot went wild, missing Margaret. Another two seconds ticked by. Pilar steadied her hand. She was determined to hit her with the next shot. She focused her sight holding a poker face and took aim a fourth time at the predator. She wanted to end this nightmare by killing this Chinese predator. She watched Margaret take aim at Ming-Li. Pilar remembered Chester telling her to always squeeze the trigger when you shoot. She carefully aimed the gun and squeezed the trigger. This time the bullet hit its target. Her eyes followed Margaret falling like a lead weight to the carpet.

Margaret moaned as she bounced on the carpet holding her stomach.

The director did not look at Admiral Mahone, but said, "Admiral, get up and run do not walk to the marine on guard duty at the gate entrance. Give him the code word, 'Tabasco.' This will tell him we need his help. Got it, Admiral. Now, move!" His eyes were focused on Margaret laying on the dining room carpet twenty feet away. He watched her face concentrate on him as she steadied her arm and lifted the revolver up from the carpet and pointed the revolver. "Don't shoot anymore, Pilar. We want her alive." The director knew from his O.S.S. days in Germany that Margaret was a rookie at shooting. A more experienced assassin would have prepared a better shot at Ming-Li.

Margaret was in terrible pain folded up on the floor. She was holding her stomach. She missed her chance to assassinate Ming-Li. She aimed the gun and squeezed the trigger. There was a loud pop from the revolver. She fired the gun at the director, who was standing twenty feet away, but the shot missed.

The director looked at Amy. He pointed at the shooter. "Amy, get the gun away from that person! " He watched Amy crawl on the carpet and grab hold of the predator's wrist pulling the gun out of the predator's hand. He turned and watched Pilar in slow motion rocket backwards over the top of her chair as her head smacked against the dining room wall. Pilar's shoulders and back slid down to collapse on the carpet. With her eyes closed, Pilar's face had no expression on her limp body. "Oh my gosh." The director saw the deadly 45-caliber bullet hit Pilar in her upper chest near her left shoulder. He realized her blood would be pouring out from the bullet wound. He grabbed a linen napkin to stop her blood from exciting the wound. The director pulled her shirt open exposing the oozing blood on her chest. He applied pressure to the wound. "Amy, get an ambulance!"

CHAPTER TWENTY-NINE

After a month-long rest and recuperation from the gunshot wound to Pilar's chest, she walked into the Cincpacflt building in Hawaii. She was greeted by an unknown second-class yeoman. He commented to Lieutenant Commander Pilar Marshall that she was needed in the conference room. As she approached the conference room, she heard familiar voices. She was taken back when she stepped into the room. To Pilar's surprise, she was greeted by Admiral Mahone, Director Von Laube, Nick and his wife, Candace and Captain Chester Marshall.

Earlier in the morning, Chester told her a white lie that this morning he had a meeting with some unknow admiral and could not go with her to meet Admiral Mahone. Pilar was happy to have her husband in the room. Pilar was thinking of resigning her naval commission and attending some university to start her MBA degree. They all saw her wide smile showing her cheery spirits.

Admiral Mahone stood up. "Welcome back, Pilar!" She offered Pilar a firm handshake. She looked at Nick. "Lieutenant J.G. McMasters, front and center."

Nick rose to stand in front of Admiral Mahone.

"McMasters, you are out of uniform."

Nick looked at his khaki shirt and looked back at the admiral.

"You have been frocked to the next officer's rank of lieutenant." She motioned to Candace to help pin the lieutenant bars on Nick's collar. "Congratulations, Lieutenant McMasters." The admiral yielded to Director Laube.

The director walked around the conference table to give Pilar a warm hug. "Good to see you, Pilar." He noticed a small tear exploding from one of her eyes. "Amy sends her best to you and so does Dusty." He placed his hand inside his suit coat jacket and pulled out a small black box. He handed the box to Pilar. He looked directly at her face and said, "This is yours, Pilar." He gently touched her shoulder. He looked at the others in the room. "Shall we get on with the ceremony?" His eyes aimed back at Pilar. "With the sincerest," he paused. "Thank you, from the United States of America for your efforts in securing a new guest to America." Everyone watched as Pilar opened the box.

Pilar's eyes froze at the medal.

"Oh, my." Pilar gazed at the Congressional Medal of Honor.

The director offered a small grin. "Pilar, we contacted the President of the United States and Ming-Li explained to him what China was planning. He has authorized me to give you this Congressional Medal of Honor for your devotion to duty. The Congressional Medal of Honor is the highest award your country can give you for valor. You might ask what is valor? Valor is boldness in the face of great danger. What is boldness? The lack of hesitation. You did not faulter in the face of danger. This award is given to you for gallantry at the risk of your life and beyond the call of duty. You placed yourself in harm's way. If it wasn't for your courage and intellect, on this assignment, Ming-Li might not have made it to her new country."

Pilar could hardly speak. She tried to say thank you in a broken course voice.

She barely got the words out of her mouth. She did not want to show any emotion. As she stood frozen in front of everyone, she raised her hand to cover her eyes. Several tears streamed down her face.

Chester quickly rose to offer her a paper napkin to dry her eyes. "I did not know you were getting this medal."

"Thank you for the napkin."

Chester whispered something in her ear. "Looks like I'll have to salute you since you are a Congressional Medal recipient."

She looked up at him and replied, "That's all-right sailor, but I love your salutes in the bedroom." She gazed into his blue eyes as she offered a partial grin. She gave him a wink from her eye. Pilar turned to look at Director Laube. "How is Dusty? Is he out of the hospital?"

"Yes, he is out of the hospital and back to working for us in Virginia." He looked at Admiral Mahone. "Can we have some cake and coffee and move on with the ceremony?"

"Of course, Director." Admiral Mahone stepped forward as Captain Marshall took his seat. "Lieutenant Commander Pilar Marshall, you are out of uniform." She watched Pilar looked over her khaki uniform.

"Yes, you are out of uniform. I notified CNO Taylor about your assignment. He was impressed with your tenacity. You have been frocked to the next highest rank of Commander. These two silver oak leaves use to be mine. I believe they gave me good fortune in my naval career." The admiral looked at Captain Marshall. "Captain, can you assist me in pinning the silver oak leaves on Pilar's collars?"

"Yes, Admiral Mahone."

Admiral Mahone and Captain Marshall removed the gold oak leaves which represented the lieutenant commander insignias and replaced them with the silver oak leaves showing everyone she was now, Commander Pilar Marshall.

"Thank you, Admiral Mahone." Pilar turned to Director Laube and asked, "What happened to the Chinese dragon, Margaret? I hope she is behind bars."

Director Laube replied, "Margaret has recovered from her stomach wound. I trust none of you get irritated at me. We convinced Margaret to work for us and she has been programed to become a double agent for us. After extensive polygraph examinations and indoctrinations on how to be a double agent, she opened up and told us about Mr. Lucky Tong, the undercover foreign Chinese agent, who runs the shoe repair shop in San Francisco. We placed in the newspaper that Ming-Li was killed, which let the Chinese know Margaret completed her assignment. The Chinese promoted Margaret to the London office. Ming-Li has a new name and we have relocated her and her mother to a new safer location. We informed Margaret the thought of being in prison for the rest of her life which grabbed her intellect and she decided to see things our way. So, if you happen to see her on the street, do not say hello or wave at her, just simply walk on by. You don't know her. Oh, one more thing, what I have told you about Margaret is top secret. Make sure you do not tell anyone of our turning her to our side." The director paused and looked at Nick's wife, Candace. "Candace, if Margaret contacts you, please get in contact with us." He watched Candace nod her head, yes. "Admiral, could someone take me to the airport?" He saw Admiral Mahone reply, yes. Director Laube turned to Pilar. "Well done, Pilar. Thank you, again for your service to our country." As he shook hands with Captain Marshall, the director leaned forward and spoke softly. "You have a great wife, Captain. She is very courageous. Few could have done this assignment with dedication to see it though as your wife did. We are very proud of her. If either of you need something," he paused for a moment, "or anything, please let me know." Director Laube turned saying his goodbyes to Nick and Candace as he exited the conference room with Admiral Mahone in tow.

Standing on the sidewalk with his hands in his pants pockets waiting for the admiral to bring the car around, Director Laube turned around and saw Pilar approaching him. "Hi Pilar. Is there something else you wanted to ask?"

"Yes, there is." Pilar waited for a moment looking down at the sidewalk and then looked at the director. "There won't be a blowback on this, will there?"

"Where did you learn this word, blowback?" "Oh, one picks up a few things along the way."

"No Pilar. There will be no blowback. Margaret has the option to easily run back to Beijing and inform her superiors she is a double agent working for the Americans and telling them Ming-Li was not killed and that the Americans lied about her death." The director pulled his hands out of his pants pockets and cleared his throat. He took hold of one of Pilar's shoulders and gently held her shoulder in the palm of his hand. He reassured her in a fatherly way. "Pilar, we have her in a box. The only way out of the box is for her to open the lid and get out of the box. This is why after World War Two, the Germans called me, Herr Umdrehen. My specialty was to turn someone around. I have a nice double-edged sword which is dangerously aimed at Margaret's carotid artery. She'll play our game and if she doesn't, Margaret will be sitting in a Chinese prison for a very long time. Yes, she loves China and hates Americans, but she loves breathing fresh air every day and being free to spend money. Right now, in our profession, she is called a painter. Margaret will paint the scenery for us in the spy business. Dusty will survey her every move. He is good at that."

Pilar watched as the director offered a small grin and then nod his head a few times cementing the truth about Margaret. She saw Admiral Mahone pull up in the black and white navy car. Pilar heard the glass door open behind her and beamed at Chester coming out of the building. She froze for a moment studying his tanned attractive face. She was lost in his eyes as he stopped. He stood next to her. She felt his hand tenderly rest on her shoulder. She was not going to let him out of her sight for the rest of the day.

As the director reached to open the car door, he glanced back at Chester and Pilar. He set his eyes on Pilar's eye-catching smooth Asian face and said, "Thanks Pilar, we will see you when time permits." With a stone-cold appearance, he offered a small wave of his hand and then turned away to enter the waiting car. He rolled down the window and eyed Pilar. He commented, "Dasvidaniya."

Pilar waived back to Director Laube as the car drove away. She turned to look at her husband and hugged him.

Chester asked, "What did he say?"

"That was odd." Pilar hesitated. "That he said that phrase in Russian, it means, 'Until we meet again'." Pilar thought for a moment as she turned toward Chester. "Something is in the air."

Chester asked, "What do you want to do now?"

"Oh, I could go shopping at the grocery store, but that's a drag. Or we could play a round of golf, but that's too labor intensive. I'm rather tired from last night. I hope I wore you out, sailor?" She gazed at him and once again looked into his steady warm blue eyes seeing infinity. Pilar could see a tiny grin appear on his handsome face. "Right now, I don't want to think. How about for the rest of the day, let's go to the beach and relax?" She grabbed his hand as they headed toward their car. "Oh, I almost forgot about the football game, Navy is playing the University of Texas, today, in Austin. I hope the Longhorns beat Navy."

One month later on a rainy afternoon from Virginia, Dusty called Pilar in Hawaii. He asked her if she ever watched John Huston's 1970 movie, *The Kremlin Letter*, which was an American espionage thriller? Dusty stated that in the movie, the actor, Richard Boone was running spy agents in Russia. At the end of the movie, there is a huge surprise.

Dusty explained to Pilar that Director Laube moved to the other side, which was a huge shock to everyone in the intelligence community. Director Laube was looked upon as a rock much like a granite rock in the intelligence society with credibility. We all trusted him. He told her, as the smoke vanishes from the flame of a fire, gone was Director Laube. Dusty informed Pilar he thought the director was on vacation. The man just disappeared. Dusty told Pilar that Director Laube is head of the Foreign Intelligence for the Russian Federation or called SVR RF. Since 1991, the SVR RF handles the intelligence and espionage functions outside the Russian Federation. The SVR RF succeeded the First Directorate to the KGB. With Director Laube as their head, he now has the capability to improve their intelligence. With his years of intelligence experience, he has the capability to really hurt us. Dusty told her that he is under investigation by the FBI and to watch her back. Before Dusty hung up the phone, he emphasized for Pilar to sit down and watch the movie. He expressed the movie will open her eyes.

ACKNOWLEDGEMENTS

This novel took numerous months to prepare each of these fictional characters into an authentic scenario . Much credit for this work is given to J. Mahone who gave me the spark to create and piece together these characters into a pragmatic tense plot. Thank you J. Mahone for the push so the book could be written. Many thanks goes to C. Marshall for the exactness of various paragraphs. Merits are given to B. Wagner and J. Emack for their additional support for the book. A shout-out is forwarded to I. Resnis for the correct course of the book. Thanks to my wife, Kathleen, for the needed assistance on the laptop computer. Thank you F. Kremer for your courageous effort as an O.S.S. officer during WW II.

A special thanks goes to Kate J. and Alexa G. for their tireless effort in getting this book printed.

The author continues to work on his wooden boat while thinking of
his next book